"Don't use force again, Joe."

Helen's voice was bitter as she warned him. "It won't work for you this time."

His hold relaxed, but he did not let her go. "I love you, Helen. I love you so much I'd do anything for you."

She shook her head, tears filming her eyes. "You'll never believe me, will you? You'll always think it's because of what you can do for me. Buying me with your wealth. What I really want is to love and be loved."

"If love is what you want, you won't get it from Max," he insisted vehemently.

"No, but I might be happy with him. I know I won't be happy with you, Joe." The tears trickled down her cheeks. "You were right the first time. You can't go back and recapture what we had. It's lost. . . ."

EMMA DARCY nearly became an actress before her fiancé declared he preferred to attend the theater with her. She became a wife and mother, but in her leisure time she managed to win many trophies in tennis. Injury forced her to limit her activities. She took up oil painting—unsuccessfully, she remarks—then architecture—she designed the family home on the Central Coast of New South Wales—and romance writing—"the hardest and most challenging of all the activities," she confesses, "but also the most rewarding, when I get it right."

Books by Emma Darcy

These books may be available at your local bookseller.

Don't miss any of our special offers. Write to us at the following address for information on our newest releases.

Harlequin Reader Service
901 Fuhrmann Blvd., P.O. Box 1397, Buffalo, NY 14240
Canadian address: P.O. Box 2800, Postal Station A,
5170 Yonge St., Willowdale, Ont. M2N 6J3

EMMA DARCY

point of impact

Harlequin Books

TORONTO • NEW YORK • LONDON
AMSTERDAM • PARIS • SYDNEY • HAMBURG
STOCKHOLM • ATHENS • TOKYO • MILAN

Harlequin Presents first edition May 1986
ISBN 0-373-10882-6

Original hardcover edition published in 1985
by Mills & Boon Limited

CHAPTER ONE

SIX-FIFTY. Only ten minutes left. Helen dragged her eyes away from the clock. The five hours had almost gone and even now she had not made up her mind. For a moment she stared blankly at the reflection in the mirror. God! What was she to do? Only gradually did her image impress itself on her fevered brain.

Stunning. She had wanted to look stunning. That's what she had told the lady in the boutique and the dress certainly achieved that objective. The cornflower blue silk was threaded with silver, the bodice cunningly pleated to shape around her full breasts and gather down a wide silver belt. It needed to be wide since the halter neckline sliced a sharp V to it, exposing a cleavage which could only be called provocative. There was no back to the dress at all, except the thin strap around her neck. The skirt hugged the generous curve of her hips before flaring down to a swinging hemline.

No bra or petticoat was possible under such a dress. Helen had drawn on an ultra-fine pair of panti-hose and strapped silver, high-heeled sandals to her feet. The whole effect was blatantly sexy, just as she had intended. But now her feet were very cold.

If she consented, could she handle it? Surely

Max would not demand too much of her. It was no love-match. But he wanted her. Oh yes, he wanted her. And female pride had demanded that he see her as the most desirable woman . . . for as long as possible . . . if she consented.

Six-fifty-four. A nervous quiver travelled down to her fingers. They trembled as she picked up the hair-brush to tidy a few wayward strands. She flicked at the bangs of hair which swept across her high, wide forehead and smoothed the sensuous fall which curved around her shoulders in a thick bob.

She put the hair-brush down and made a last appraisal of her appearance. The full-lipped mouth curved into a grimace. The 'golden girl' tag would seem appropriate to anyone seeing her tonight. The golden hair shimmered like silk, the golden-tan skin was very much in evidence, and there was no blemish on the beauty which had won that title four years ago. The perfect balance of her face would never change. Good bone structure ensured that. Perhaps her figure was a little fuller than in her modelling days, but the extra inches added a more womanly proportion to her above-average height.

Six-fifty-seven. She picked up her silver evening-bag and walked out to the living-room. Max would be here any minute. The decision had to be made. Now. Her eyes flicked around the room, vaguely seeking an answer which could only be found in her own mind.

It was a room full of possessions, pleasant and

comfortable with its thick, honey-coloured carpet and armchairs upholstered in cinnamon velvet, yet at this moment it seemed to hold a terrible emptiness. Helen's gaze sought an emotional reassurance from the shelves of books, the souvenirs from other countries, all the things which measured some part of her life.

Her eyes fastened inexorably on the cheapest possession of all. The little china clown looked out of place in this room but only it held meaning. Too much meaning. An ever-present reminder of intense pleasure and pain. Almost against her will Helen was drawn to it. Her fingers closed around it, caressing its simple contours. The one gift of love, given her on a day when she and Joe had been so happy together. So in love. Bubbling over with it. The only real love she had ever had and even that she had been unable to keep.

Pain crept over the memory, just as it always did. Her fingers tightened. She sucked in a deep breath and thrust the clown back on its shelf. Joe was gone. He would never come back to her. The years had hammered that point into her heart. And in four long years of loneliness, Max was the only man who had come to mean anything at all to her. It was time to give up dreaming and face up to reality. The love she once had, was lost to her forever, and this last year with Max had been good.

His flowers beckoned her to the coffee-table. The extravagant arrangement was typical of the

man. He did everything with style. A central peak
of tall daffodils nodded down to a skirting of blue
and yellow irises which were surrounded by masses
of violets. She read the accompanying card again.

'To my golden girl, whose blue eyes are more
bewitching than flowers. May our life be a bed of
violets, but not of the shrinking kind. Be bold,
sweet maid, and let who will be run-of-the-mill.'

Bold or foolhardy? One thing was certain. Life
with one of the most successful entrepreneurs in
Australia was never going to be run-of-the-mill.
She knew he had hired her as a public relations
frontispiece for his operations, with the secondary
consideration of getting her into his bed, but she
had earned his respect by her handling of
important clients with firm tact and authority,
and by determinedly meeting every responsibility
he handed her. And perhaps her refusal to
occupy his bed on the casual basis he persistently
offered had won another kind of respect too.

Not that he had ever pressed her hard. That
was not his way. Easy-come, easy-go was Max's
motto where women were concerned. His speech
fell naturally into a sexual banter when any
woman was around. He was a playboy through
and through but he did not play with work.

Max gave all of himself to work, relishing its
challenges and riding high on success. She did
too. And this they shared ... intimately. But
would that bond be worn thin or strengthened by
the even greater intimacy of marriage ... twenty-
four hours a day?

Helen sighed, all too aware that she wanted, needed love. Yet she despaired of love ever coming her way again. If she married Max, surely her life with him would be better than this loneliness. Her happiest hours were when she was at work. With him.

The doorbell rang.

With a heavy sense of fate Helen went to admit the man who was expecting her answer.

Max smiled at her. He looked rakishly handsome in his royal blue velvet jacket and frilled shirt. The wavy black hair, arched eyebrows and the strong, slightly hooked nose, white teeth against a darkly tanned skin; they all added up to a piratical charm which was well-nigh irresistible. He was a tall man whose lean frame emanated a dynamic energy and he carried an aura of excitement which was infectious.

'Not only beautiful, but bountiful,' he declared, his dark eyes aglow with open admiration.

'Bountiful?' Helen queried, holding off the moment of surrender even now.

Max's smile grew into a grin. 'There isn't anything you haven't got. All the goodies in one package, so to speak.'

Her answering smile held a slight twist of irony. 'I'd like to think so, Max. Thanks for the lovely flowers. Do you want to come in? I bought a bottle of Pol Roger to toast your birthday.'

'Ah, the king of champagnes!' he pronounced and stepped inside, pushing the door shut behind him. 'I was right to ask you to marry me. You know all my vices.'

She laughed. 'Oh, I think you have a few virtues too.'

He caught her as she was about to turn away and pulled her into a loose embrace, his eyes questioning seriously. 'I hope that means what I want it to mean.'

This was the moment. Helen quelled the last second flutter of doubt. The steady blue eyes denied any uncertainty as she returned his gaze. 'The answer's yes, Max. I will marry you.'

It was done. For better or for worse the decision had been made.

Max gathered her closer to him. 'That's the best gift of all,' he murmured, his tone and touch surprisingly gentle.

Helen tried not to tense up but she could not keep relaxed enough to deceive Max.

'I'm not going to rush you into bed, Helen,' he assured her kindly. 'Give me credit for some sensitivity. Besides, anticipation always enhances pleasure.' His eyes drifted down the inviting cleavage of her dress and fingertips lightly teased the edge of silk, pausing in the soft valley between her breasts. He lifted a gaze rich with satisfaction. 'You wore this dress for me?'

'Yes.' The word was barely a whisper. She did not know if it was fear or excitement driving her heart to pound so wildly but her eyes obviously mirrored something of what she felt.

'Don't be afraid. I won't give you any reason to

regret the confidence you've placed in me,' Max said softly and lifted his hand to stroke her cheek in almost a gesture of tenderness before tilting her chin for his kiss ... their very first ... a seal of commitment.

Helen made a conscious effort to surrender her mouth to him but little effort was required under Max's sensual persuasion. His kiss left her with a heightened sense of excitement and very aware that his strong masculinity had awakened an instinctive response in her body. Some of her fearful uncertainty receded.

Max's grin held a boyish look of mischief. 'You know something, Helen? Much as I want you, what I'm looking forward to most is the moment when that awesome control of yours breaks and I get to see what really lies behind the enigmatic composure you've kept in place ever since I've known you.'

Her laugh was a little shaky. 'Maybe I shall hang on to it since it serves to keep your interest.'

Max chuckled at her reply, all too sure of his power to arouse her now that she had given in to him. And he was right. Even now her blood was tingling under the skin where his seductive touch had lingered.

'You won't lose my interest, Helen,' he assured her. 'You're a many-faceted jewel, not a pretty piece of glass. Which reminds me. We'll go shopping for a ring tomorrow.'

'Very traditional of you, Max. Do you really want to?' she tilted at him, composure restored by breaking away and heading for the refrigerator. She handed him the chilled bottle of Pol Roger to open.

'I'm not averse to tradition. When it suits me. And I have a fancy to give you pleasure.' He grinned at her as he popped the cork. 'Lots of pleasure.'

She smiled. 'I had a fancy to give you pleasure too. See what I bought you for your birthday?' She held out the delicately carved Lalique glasses. 'I thought you'd like the winged lady motif.'

He took one and handled it appreciatively before giving her a look of immense gratification. 'You're also a woman of exquisite taste. Thank you, Helen.' He poured champagne into the glasses and held his up to the light. The carved wings stood out in sharp relief on the delicate crystal and the lady's face at the base of the goblet glowed with liquid gold. 'Beautiful!' He gestured a toast. 'To us and our partnership! A brilliant connection, even though I say it myself.'

She sipped the champagne, conscious of a heady exhilaration. Max's confidence boosted hers and it was very pleasant to bask in the warmth of his gaze, knowing that he not only wanted but appreciated her also. 'When do you want to get married, Max?'

'We'll have a couple of weeks free after the Joel Thomas tour. How about then?' he answered matter-of-factly.

She nodded and motioned him out of the

kitchen and into her living-room. She paused at the coffee-table to admire the flowers again. 'I'll have to notify my landlord,' she murmured, thinking ahead to all the packing which would have to be done, arrangements to be made. Six more weeks here and her single life would be over.

Max had moved up behind her. He bent his head and grazed his lips over one bare shoulder. 'Move in with me tomorrow.'

Her skin prickled with sensitivity. 'No. When we're married, Max. Not before,' she said decisively, then added on a softer, more whimsical note, 'I'm a bit of a traditionalist myself.'

Fingertips trailed down the curve of her spine. She shivered.

'Maybe I can change your mind about that,' Max murmured suggestively.

Maybe he could, she thought wildly. He was awakening her body to a physical awareness which she had not known for a long time. 'And maybe we'd better get going if we're not to arrive late,' she answered huskily.

His fingers continued to tantalise nerve-endings. 'Your skin is like silk.'

'Max!' She turned on him, a hint of panic in her voice.

Again his grin was mischievous but there was a gleam of exultation in his eyes. 'You know I find it quite incredible that this is the same cool Helen Daley I've worked with all year.'

Cool! She was far from cool but she arched a

mocking eyebrow. 'Self-defence. The job was too important to me to put it at risk by getting our work relationship muddled. It's the only job I've had that uses all of me, not just trading on my looks. I'd had three years of being "the golden girl" and believe me, I hated it.'

He frowned in self-annoyance. 'I'm sorry. I hadn't realised you hated it. I'll never use the term again.'

She made a quick, dismissive gesture. 'It doesn't matter. I don't let any of that touch me any more.'

Max eyed her consideringly. 'You don't let much touch you at all, do you, Helen?'

I did once, she thought to herself. Four years ago. When Nell Daley died. And was buried under a tombstone called 'the golden girl'. Helen pushed away the morbid thought and gave a light reply. 'When people only see you as a surface you learn to live within yourself. Other women don't want to get close to me . . .'

Max nodded understanding. 'You outshine them.'

'. . . and men only want one kind of closeness,' she finished sardonically.

'So you closed in on yourself.'

She smiled appreciation of the quip. 'It's a rather lonely life.'

'Yes, damnably lonely.'

The muttered comment raised Helen's eyebrows. Max, lonely? Surely his tightly packed social life left him little time for loneliness.

His eyes gently mocked her. 'That shouldn't surprise you, Helen. You, more than anyone, can appreciate the truth that surface relationships don't satisfy. I've had more satisfaction out of our platonic relationship than I've had from any other woman in years.'

Helen felt enormously pleased. 'Thank you, Max. I haven't had a nicer compliment since I left university.'

He shook his head in bemusement. 'I know you told me you studied economics but damned if I can see you swotting over dry statistics. I'm glad you went into modelling since it brought you to my notice, but just as a point of idle curiosity, why did you enter that beauty contest if you didn't want what it led to?'

Her pleasure faded as the old pain once more clutched her heart. 'I had a need for approval,' she said with bleak self-knowledge, then tried to shrug the memory away, deliberately injecting a lighter note into her voice. 'I was young and stupid. And once it was done I found I couldn't go back to what I'd had before.'

There was no twinkle at all in Max's eyes as he murmured, 'No, you can't go back.' He seemed to force a smile. 'But we do have now, and I approve of you, Helen. You know that, don't you?'

She put a smile on her face too. 'Yes. It's what I like about you. Among other things,' she added teasingly.

He grinned, and whatever introspection had

shadowed his eyes was dismissed. The devilment was back. 'We'll get to those other things later. Finish your champagne. We'll take the bottle with us and drink the rest on the way.'

Helen carried the empty glasses to the kitchen. She automatically rinsed them and left them on the draining-board. Max would be returning to the apartment with her later. She would replace them in their box and give them to him when he left again. She picked up her evening-bag and joined him at the front-door. His smile and the possessive way he took her arm warmed her heart. She felt more confident of the rightness of her decision as they walked downstairs.

'Why did you ask me today, Max?' she asked curiously. 'I mean why today? There's always a reason behind your timing.'

He laughed. 'You know me too well, Helen. I wanted to make the announcement tonight.'

'What if I'd said no?'

'Then there wouldn't have been an announcement.'

The question still tickled. He had not fully answered it. 'What's so special about tonight? I know it's your birthday, but . . .'

'I enjoy presenting the unexpected. Madeleine undoubtedly expects to get a story for her column out of this birthday party or she wouldn't have arranged it. But she won't be anticipating this story.'

His smile denied the faint twist of malice in the words but Helen's ears were attuned to it. For some reason Madeleine Kane got to Max, like a burr under his skin. The relationship between columnist and entrepreneur was an odd one. They did each other favours. Inside stories on visiting stars were traded for good publicity. Yet Helen was sure there was no love lost between them. Their conversation was always a running duel, thrust, parry, counter-thrust, as if under the veneer of cosy friendship they were really bitter antagonists.

But then Madeleine Kane was hardly sweet to anyone. Every time she telephoned for Max she invariably called Helen 'Miss World' or 'Miss Universe' in that tone of fine contempt she did so well. It was like water off a duck's back to Helen. She had long ago learnt to deflect the bitchy barbs from other women by using a cool politeness that gave them no satisfaction.

The white Rolls Royce stood at the kerb. Max's chauffeur, Barry Weber was at the passenger door, ready to hand them in. Max had a stable of cars which Barry looked after with enormous pride. The Rolls was his favourite and was always used for big occasions. Barry saw them settled into the back seat and took the wheel. The glass partition was up. Max opened the bar compartment and proceeded to pour the champagne into more glasses.

'Has Madeleine mentioned whom she's bringing to the party?' Helen asked, her curiosity aroused by the woman despite the antagonism she invariably projected. Madeleine Kane was a

self-proclaimed single person who was somewhat
notorious as a manhunter.

Max's mouth curled with distaste as he handed
Helen her glass. 'No doubt she will have
prepared her own little surprise. I don't know
who, but you can be sure it'll be someone new
and someone she can use in one way or another.
Madeleine has no heart.'

The bitter edge to that last comment reinforced
Helen's private opinion that Max had once been
emotionally involved with Madeleine. The elec-
tricity that crackled between them could not have
originated from a merely physical affair and their
association went back a long way, back beyond
Caroline.

Caroline. Max's ex-wife. His first marriage had
only lasted three weeks. Helen gnawed over that
irrefutable fact for several moments, then felt
impelled to speak. 'Max, you are serious about
our marriage, aren't you? I mean . . .' She faltered
and flushed, not wanting to refer to Caroline. Her
mind snatched at Jimmy Danvers as an example.
The radio-chat man would be at the party tonight
with his third wife. 'I wouldn't like to be thought
of as expendable as Jimmy's wives.'

Max's steady gaze was reassuring. 'Helen, if I
were not serious, I would not have proposed.
And you're wrong about Jimmy, you know. Each
time he's married, he's been in love with the
woman and has thought it would last. He's an
incurable romantic,' he added drily.

'And you're not.'

He smiled. 'Do you want me to be?'

She shook her head. 'I like it how it is between us. Straight honesty.'

'So do I. If I hadn't met you I'd probably have continued on like Keith. I doubt he'll ever marry again.'

Most unlikely, Helen thought derisively. Keith bought women as he wanted them. A millionaire many times over, Keith Farrell was THE advertising man, although his business interests ranged far and wide. Jill Amory was his companion of the moment and both of them were guests at the party tonight.

Max leaned over and squeezed her hand. 'Stop worrying. Look at Bart and Penny. They've been married fifteen years and I'm sure their lasting power comes from working together. Like us.'

Helen relaxed. Max was surely right about Bart and Penny Chissolm. The highly rated comedians kept a united front in public whatever private differences they had. She was glad they would be at the party. They were always good fun.

'Helen, this is no spur-of-the-moment decision on my part,' Max assured her, apparently concerned about her disquiet. 'I wouldn't have considered a marriage with you if I thought divorce was just around the corner. That's not how you think, is it?'

'No,' she admitted with a rueful smile. 'My parents were divorced. I don't want that for myself.'

'Bad time?' he murmured sympathetically.

The past had already intruded too much tonight. She shrugged it away, determined to be happy with Max. 'That was a long time ago. I haven't seen my father since I was ten. And I think my mother was relieved to see me leave home as soon as I finished school. Her remarriage had made me a surplus item.'

The dry twist she gave the last words brought a chuckle from Max. 'The new husband had an eye for the daughter?'

She rolled her eyes at him, making light of what had been a miserable time in her life. 'Do you always convert everything to the physical?'

He shook his head, his eyes laughing at her. 'Helen, any man who didn't want you would have to be blind. I'm going to be a much-envied man and knowing that you're now mine makes me feel very proud.'

He took her empty glass, replaced it in the bar compartment, then drew her arm through his with a smug air of ownership. 'In fact, you've made me feel a new man tonight. Life is going to be worth living with you.'

She smiled up at him, feeling more content with her decision. Max's assurances had quietened her doubts and even though there was no love between them, the future was looking better all the time.

Barry slid the Rolls to a gentle halt at Circular Quay. He was a likeable young man who really enjoyed his job, wearing his chauffeur's uniform with pride and performing all services with the style he considered appropriate. The Rolls Royce invariably brought out the ham in him, and tonight as he held the door open for Helen and Max to alight, Helen suspected he could barely restrain himself from giving a salute. Her smile broke into a giggle as they walked down the quay to where the *Kukuni Queen* was berthed.

'What's amusing you?' Max queried.

'Barry. I thought he was going to burst his brass buttons, his chest was puffed out so much.'

Max chuckled. 'He does it well though.'

'Oh, he's priceless, Max! I love him.'

The brown eyes caressed her with a warmth which stripped her light mood. 'You're the one who's priceless, Helen. And tonight I'd prefer it to be me you love.'

Her heart gave a sick little lurch. She chided herself for the reaction and took a deep, steadying breath. She had known how the night would end once she had given her consent. Max was a very experienced lover. As a matter of pride or ego, call it what you will, he would undoubtedly use all his sexual expertise to give her pleasure tonight. She had nothing to fear on that score. But would it be enough! It had to be. The commitment had been made.

They had reached the gang-plank. Max guided her up with assiduous care. The *Kukuni Queen* was a retired Manly ferry which had been refurbished into a floating restaurant. Not only did it boast a superb cuisine and select cellar, but it promoted romance on a grand scale; polished decks for dancing under the stars, a small orchestra, a dining-room of quiet elegance, and the most magnificent setting of all with the beauty of Sydney Harbour on all sides.

The Captain met them on deck, his gaze clinging to Helen as he wished them a pleasant evening and passed them on to the Head Waiter who found it equally difficult to stop his eyes from feasting on her even while he addressed Max.

'Ah, Mr Abrams! Your party is all on board. In fact, sir, you're the last couple to arrive. We'll be leaving the Quay in five minutes. Should be a beautiful evening for you. No clouds in the sky. No wind. Full moon. Oh, and our cellar-master has managed to get hold of a '53 Lafite.'

'Has he? Splendid chap! We shall certainly indulge ourselves tonight,' Max declared with relish. 'He couldn't get hold of a '45 Mouton?'

The answering shrug was expressive. 'He did his best. There was none available. But . . .'

Helen switched off. Her knowledge of wine was very limited. The Head Waiter was only too eager to carry on the conversation. His gaze flicked again and again to Helen, despite her silence on the subject. Max was not offended. He enjoyed the attention she automatically drew. And Helen was not offended either. She had put herself on show tonight, pandering to Max's ego, and no-one else mattered. She was pleasing him. The man to whom she had now linked her life.

When they moved into the dining-room she

was aware of heads turning their way and knew
Max was savouring the impact of their entrance
on the other diners. Max was a showman to his
fingertips. With an indifference born from having
been subjected to too many stares, Helen was
able to ignore the eyes which were dissecting her.
She looked ahead to their table and began
checking over the identities of those already
seated.

Madeleine Kane was leaning forward, obscuring the features of her escort. The columnist
was wearing a tightly fitting black dress which
did not flatter her thinness or her bony shoulders.
Not that Madeleine would care. In fact she
seemed to go out of her way to emphasise
physical defects, arrogantly denying them any
importance. Her red hair was piled into a loose
concoction on top of her head, precariously held
by several jewelled combs.

Helen noticed Jill Amory's fawning manner as
she stroked Keith Farrell's arm. His wide mouth
was set in its habitual sardonic curl. Bart and
Penny Chissolm seemed to be arguing. Jimmy
Danvers caught Helen's eye and gave a cheery
wave, alerting Madeleine to their arrival. She
swivelled around to face them, an amused smile
on her lips.

The profile of her partner carved its familiar
lines out of Helen's memory, starting off a scream
of protest which shrieked around her brain. No!
It couldn't be. Not Joe. Not here. Not now.

'What is it?' Max murmured.

He had stopped their walk. She looked at him, eyes blank with shock, aware that he had spoken yet slow to register his words. His frown prompted an answer.

'Nothing. It's nothing,' she choked out.

His smile was very dry. 'Then why are you digging your nails into my hand?'

She looked down in dismay. The imprint of her nails was quite clear. 'I'm sorry. I didn't mean to do that.'

'What's the matter, Helen?'

The matter? Joe Torelli was seated at their table. That was the matter. And she did not want to face him. Her whole being revolted against the situation. But she could not say that.

'I . . . I guess I feel nervous, Max. Do we have to make the announcement tonight?' she blurted out in a rush of panic.

'Why not?'

Why not indeed? Why should Joe make any difference? He was with Madeleine. In four years he had made no attempt to contact Helen. But, oh God! What malevolent coincidence had brought him here tonight to confuse her like this?

'Not having second thoughts, are you, Helen?'

Yes, her heart screamed. No, her mind insisted. Joe was the past. Max was the present.

'No, of course not,' she said with a semblance of her former composure. She forced a smile to her lips. 'I'm all right now. It's just that they're your old friends and they must remember Caroline.'

Max squeezed her hand reassuringly. 'Caroline

is way, way in the past, Helen. You're the woman
for me.'

And you're the man for me, Helen assured
herself as convincingly as she could. Not Joe. Joe
could only hurt her. But she wished he wasn't
here. It wasn't fair that fate should play her such
a dirty trick tonight. Oh God! It wasn't fair!
Hadn't she agonised enough over her decision. It
was made now and there was no going back. No
going back to what she and Joe had once shared.
It just wasn't fair that he was here to remind her.

They resumed their approach to the table, Max
tucking her arm into his possessively. Madeleine's
lips moved in some little aside to Joe. The dark
head turned. There was no surprise or shock in
the eyes which met Helen's. He had either known
she was coming or simply did not care. Why
should he care, Helen reasoned, trying desperately
to match his air of disinterest.

It was difficult enough that she should meet
him like this, but to find him with Madeleine
Kane . . . dear God! That hurt. That really hurt.
Madeleine only paraded men who were her
lovers. Apart from her reputation and her cruel
tongue, the woman had to be at least six years
older than Joe. Somehow that made their
connection even more sordid.

The tall redhead rose to her feet, her green
eyes glinting with the same malicious anticipation
which Max had shown earlier. They slid over
Helen with barely an acknowledgement before
fixing on her target.

'Max, darling,' she purred, bright red finger-nails digging into his velvet sleeves with feline pleasure. 'So handsome tonight. Why, no-one would ever know you were a year closer to your grave. Should I offer felicitations or commiserations for this birthday. Or maybe thirty-six kisses to make you feel the passing years were all worth it.' She leaned forward and planted a smacking kiss on his cheek.

'One of those is more than sufficient, Madeleine,' he drawled, making a deliberate point of wiping off her lipstick with his handkerchief. 'Felicitations are always pleasant, particularly when you give them so gracefully, but tonight it would please me to hear your congratulations.'

She arched her eyebrows then wrinkled her forehead in mock dismay. 'Oh dear! Is each year becoming so difficult for you, Max?'

'Not at all, my dear Madeleine. They fly by too quickly and I intend to make the most of those remaining.'

His gaze swept around the table commanding everyone's attention. Helen did not know where to look. Impossible to even glance in Joe's direction. She fixed her eyes on Cheryl Danvers whose mouth was slightly open, waiting expectantly for Max to continue. Which he did. Inevitably.

'In fact, you may all congratulate me ... and my wife-to-be. Helen and I are getting married.'

CHAPTER TWO

THE stunned silence was all Max could have wished. He had presented the unexpected all right. Cheryl Danvers' mouth dropped even further open.

Helen found the silence excruciating. It tore at nerves which were already stretched to snapping point. She wished someone would say something, anything. She desperately needed a cloak of normality to hide her emotional turmoil. Her eyes darted around, almost begging for a word, a remark, any little pleasantry.

Jill Amory's surprise was mixed with envy. Keith Farrell's eyes were narrowed speculatively. Penny and Bart Chissolm were pulling faces at each other, goggling caricatures of disbelief. Helen's gaze was inexorably drawn to Joe.

His eyes were downcast, apparently staring at the glass of wine in his hand. His thumb flicked sharply, making a pinging sound against the crystal. What was he thinking? Was he remembering the marriage they had planned together? Did he regret their parting? Helen derided herself for the futile speculation. Their relationship was four years dead and there never had been any hope of its resurrection. Now she was going to marry Max. And Joe was with Madeleine Kane.

'We seem to have struck the company dumb, Helen,' Max drawled, but there was a note of exultation in the dry tone. 'Do you suppose it's because I had the effrontery to ask you, or that you had the courage to accept me?'

She forced an equally dry comment to her tongue. 'Perhaps it's a bold choice for both of us.'

Max chuckled over her emphasis on the word he had used in his note.

'Well, I think it's marvellous!' Cheryl Danvers proclaimed in her vacuous way.

'Hear, hear! Congratulations, you old rake! Met your match at last,' Jimmy crowed.

Keith Farrell couldn't resist a light jibe. 'One hell of a way to celebrate your birthday, Max. I wish you luck.'

Bart and Penny Chissolm chorussed boisterous congratulations and Max accepted them with obvious pleasure. Helen forced a smile. Joe offered no comment. For which she was grateful since her teeth would probably gnash if he uttered one word of well-wishing.

'Madeleine . . .' It was a prompt from Max.

Like Joe, she had remained silent. Helen turned her attention to the tall redhead who stood on the other side of Max. The mobile face was curiously still, the white skin almost translucent, but the green eyes were alive and venomous with hatred. And the hatred was directed straight at Helen, a deadly shaft that wished its victim in hell.

Helen stared back at her, shocked by the naked emotion. There was a subtle shift in the dangerous glitter and a veil of mockery masked the hatred. The thin red lips stretched into a smile as Madeleine lifted her face to Max.

'So kind of you to share your news with us, Max, but I can't say it's really surprising. You run so true to form. Two brides . . . two beauty queens. A pity that Helen is something of a has-been. You should have married her four years ago when she won the title . . . as you did with Caroline.'

The honeyed bitchiness dripped from her tongue with sadistic control, making each point a telling one. Helen felt the hot rush of blood up her throat and could do nothing to stop its spread across her cheeks. If Joe had not been present, Madeleine's darts would not have been so poisonous. It had been the beauty title which had finished Helen and Joe. The last straw.

'However . . .' she continued, 'the announcement of your engagement might stir some interest and speculation among my readers. Now, let me introduce a new friend of mine, Joe?'

No time to recover. With her cheeks burning there was no other course for Helen but to brazen out the inevitable introduction. She looked unflinchingly at Joe, determined to act with polite detachment.

He rose to his feet with the confident air of a man who kow-towed to no one. He seemed to be more handsome than she remembered. His face was not so thin and there was a greater width of shoulder and chest. He had filled out, become a man who seemed completely sure of himself. The formal black dinner suit sat well on him, somehow placing him a cut above Max in his more theatrical clothes.

'Max, Helen, I'd like you to meet Joe Torelli.'

Helen took the hand which was offered to her. His touch sent a tingle of awareness right up her arm but she managed to speak in a casual tone.

'Hello, Joe.'

'Nell . . .' He pressed her fingers lightly but there was no flicker of memory in his voice or on his face. Both were curiously expressionless.

'You two know each other?' Max queried.

'Yes. We were at university together,' Helen replied matter-of-factly.

'Before Nell became a beauty queen and turned into Helen of Troy.' The remark was spoken in a soft, low tone, edged with a trace of contempt.

It was all Helen could do not to snatch her hand away. He was good at hurting. Just as good as Madeleine. They were a fine pair. A shadow of the old despair squeezed her heart. Not even the wholehearted gift of her body had been enough to convince Joe that she loved him, and only him. She had been naïve to believe it would since it was her body that had caused all the trouble between them. Even now it had provoked a jibe.

The hand was withdrawn and offered to Max who took it affably enough, but there was a look of hard assessment in the older man's eyes which belied the ready smile on his lips.

'At university, eh?' The smile took on a sardonic curl. 'My dear Madeleine, I didn't realise you took such an interest in the promising youth of our country.' The emphasis on youth was a barely veiled barb.

'You are mistaken, Max. Again. Joe doesn't promise. He delivers. Straight down the line with no devious little hops elsewhere. I find that rather refreshing, don't you? And you know what else strikes me about Joe?'

'Apart from being young and refreshing?' Max drawled mockingly.

'Not apart from. Because of it. You see, Max, Joe looks and acts very much as you did when you were ten years younger. The cast of your features is so similar you could be brothers. Don't you think so, Helen?'

It was true. The likeness hit her with sickening force. Joe's black hair was curlier, his eyebrows less arched than Max's but the dark eyes were very similar. And the noses ... Max's Jewish nose having the same hawkish look of Joe's Italian heritage. Both mouths were shaped with full sensuous lips. They were tall, lean men.

A terrible chill crept into Helen's heart. Was this why she had been physically attracted to Max? She had tried to block Joe out of her mind but now it seemed that her subconscious had been looking for a replacement. The awful part

was, now that the comparison had been made, she
was unlikely to forget it.

'Well? Have I struck you dumb, Helen?' came
the silky taunt from Madeleine.

'There is a resemblance,' she answered flatly.

Max did not like it. Madeleine had scored a hit.
His voice was altogether too silky as he remarked,
'Well, Joe, all I can do is offer you my sympathy.
If Madeleine ever mistakes you for me, that
young skin of yours will be clawed into shreds.
She likes to sharpen her talons on me but luckily
I have grown a tough old hide.'

'I doubt she'll make that mistake.' Joe replied
with a touch of arrogance.

'Then enjoy her high regard while you can,
dear boy,' Max said with sweet condescension.
He slid an arm around Helen's shoulders and
smiled. 'I am so very happy tonight, I would
wish everyone to share the same happiness. Shall
we sit down?'

The brief flare of hatred in the green eyes
showed that Max had evened the score. Helen's
intuition had been right. There was a deep,
personal grudge between Max and Madeleine and
the daggers were out tonight with a vengeance.
Helen was glad to sit down. Shocks had come
thick and fast and she felt weak from the
pummelling her heart had taken.

Jimmy Danvers welcomed her into the seat
next to him. Max took the head of the table on
her left. Joe helped Madeleine to the place
opposite Helen and resumed his own seat next to

her. The red fingernails ran down his sleeve and stroked his hand.

Helen's skin crawled. The thought of those nails caressing Joe's skin, of Joe in Madeleine's bed making love as he had made love to Helen . . . Stop it! she commanded herself fiercely. She had to shut those memories out, keep them blocked. Talk, do something, but don't remember. She looked down to the other end of the table, seeking distraction.

Keith Farrell caught her eye and smiled his know-it-all smile. He was a big man with a fleshy face. His florid complexion was broken by sharp blue eyes and topped with thinning, sandy hair. Helen did not like him and he knew it.

'What a dark horse you are, Max!' Penny Chissolm remarked teasingly. 'I never thought you'd enter the marriage stakes again.'

'But the palomino wins,' Keith put in slyly, his eyes holding Helen's with mocking intent. 'So, the golden girl can say yes . . . for the right price.'

Helen gritted her teeth. The urge to spit at Keith Farrell was almost overwhelming, but now, more than at any other moment in her life, the need to stay poised and in control was paramount. Pride and self-respect demanded that his insinuation be not only rebutted but completely killed.

'It has always surprised me that a man of your business acumen could not see past the "golden girl" label, Keith,' she said lightly, then projected a telling warmth into her voice. 'The reason why

Max is so special to me is that he doesn't see me with your eyes.'

She turned a glowing smile to Max, aware that she had drawn everyone's attention. 'He's the only man I've ever known who accepts me as the person I am.' Her gaze swept slowly around the table, determined to impress each person, including Joe ... especially Joe ... with the sincerity of her feeling. 'And once we're married, the person I am will stand by him through sickness and in health, for better or worse, richer or poorer, because that's what the commitment of marriage means to me.'

Madeleine gave a slow hand-clap. 'A very pretty speech, my dear.' Her smile was positively scintillating. 'And do you expect the same stalwart devotion from Max?'

Helen ignored the mocking lilt and replied with a cool edge of warning. 'I speak for myself, Madeleine. I wouldn't want Max's friends to have any misunderstanding about where I stand. I wouldn't want anything to upset the cordial relationships you've always shared. As Max's wife, I would hope you will all accept me as a friend too ...' She shot a significant look at Keith. '... and not regard me as a label.'

It was gratifying to find a grudging respect in the pale blue eyes. Keith surprised Helen even further by lifting his glass to her.

'Wise men make mistakes. Fools repeat them. I, for one, do not repeat mistakes.' His sardonic little smile came into play. 'As a man who does pride himself on possessing considerable business acumen, I rue the fact that you did not take the time to correct me before tonight, and I hope you'll overlook my error of judgment. I wish you both well.' He raised his glass higher. 'To Helen and Max . . .'

The toast was echoed around the table. Max reached over and took Helen's hand, lifting it on to the table in a proud show of ownership. There was pride in his eyes too, not the pride he had shown in her appearance but a much deeper, warmer admiration and pleasure than he had ever shown her before, and his voice held an uncharacteristic note of tenderness when he spoke, addressing her as well as the company.

'And let me say that I consider myself a very lucky man indeed, that Helen has decided to bestow this hand on me. To my mind, she is unique.'

He lifted it higher and brushed his lips reverently across her knuckles. Tears of gratitude pricked Helen's eyes. It was the support she had needed and Max had given it handsomely. There was a chorus of approval from most of the others but not from Madeleine and not from Joe.

But Helen had recovered her composure now. And her confidence. She was with Max, secure in her position at his side and not a person to be intimidated by anyone here. She had long since stopped being the vulnerable girl Joe had crushed, and years of experience had taught her

how to handle men like Keith, and women like
Madeleine.

She lifted a defiant gaze to the woman
opposite, challenging Madeleine to do her worst,
but the green eyes were downcast, seemingly
mesmerised by the movement of Max's thumb.
He had retained possession of Helen's hand and
was stroking her wrist, back and forth, back and
forth in a slow, deliberate caress. Madeleine's
thin face looked gaunt, the skin so pale as to be
almost sickly.

Did she want Max, Helen wondered? Was that
the cause of her hatred towards me? But Madeleine
had Joe, came the swift contradiction, and Helen
steeled herself to look at the man she had loved. His
face also seemed pale, with tight lines around the
mouth as if the toast he had drunk had been sour to
his taste. His hooded gaze was fixed on the glass in
front of him which he was slowly revolving
between index finger and thumb.

Madeleine suddenly snapped back to life. She
leaned towards Joe and the red fingernails slid
over his shoulder and tickled his ear. She pouted
flirtatiously.

'Joe, darling, Max and Helen are making me
feel all romantic. Doesn't it get to you too?'

Was there an infinitesimal pause before he
turned his head? An effort made? No. He slid too
quickly into his role. He grinned and playfully bit
Madeleine's fingers. She laughed and tapped him
on the cheek with the kind of indulgence which
said 'good boy'.

'Watch yourself, Madeleine,' he said in a mock growl. 'I can bite harder than that.'

'A real tiger,' she purred.

Helen felt sick. Fortunately a drink waiter descended on them with a wine-list which he handed to Max and a serviette-shrouded bottle from which he proceeded to top up their glasses with champagne. Never before had Helen needed a drink so much. It would be lucky if she retained her surface composure, she thought bitterly. Even with Max at her side she could not stomach the idea of Joe with Madeleine.

It seemed that Max had not cared for that little display of intimacy either. 'Would you like to choose a wine, Joe?' he offered smoothly, holding out the list with a smile of subtle challenge. The old tiger was about to show off his stripes.

Joe laughingly demurred. 'When it comes to choosing wines I am a complete novice, Max. I bow to your experience.'

The smile quirked sardonically. 'But not a novice in other fields, I'll warrant.'

'One tends to specialise these days,' came the casual answer.

'Oh? And what do you specialise in?'

'Pleasing me,' Madeleine put in wickedly.

'Why, Madeleine, you surprise me,' Max said in his most urbane manner. 'I didn't think you'd need to stoop to a gigolo.'

Helen's eyes flew in horror to Joe, expecting him to explode. She still had emotional scars from that volatile male pride. Never, never would he accept any form of financial support from a woman, not even the woman he was marrying. Her eyes widened in astonishment as an amused smile curved his lips.

'Madeleine? A gigolo?' he mocked. 'You've got to be joking, Max. She is, without a doubt, the most fascinating woman I've ever met. I'd pay to have her company, as I imagine a lot of men would.' He took a stray lock of the bright red hair and tucked it behind her ear as he bent towards it and murmured suggestively, 'Are you for sale, Madeleine?'

She laughed up at him. 'No, my pet. I have to be earned. Occasionally, when the mood takes me, I give myself away ... like Max.' Her gaze quickly sliced back to feed off Max's reaction.

He lifted one eyebrow in studied disdain. 'You think me more generous than I am, Madeleine. I rarely give unless I see a profit in the gift.'

The green eyes moved to Helen, stabbing her with vicious mockery. 'I think there's a lesson in there somewhere for you, my dear. You've gone very silent. Overcome with happiness?'

'I'm listening, Madeleine,' Helen said with more bite than she intended. 'I'm very good at listening ... and observing. That's why Max and I work so well together.'

'Ah yes! But does the right hand know what the left hand is doing?' came the sly retort.

Helen answered with sweet reason. 'If both belong to the same body then they're working in a common interest, wouldn't you say?'

So swallow that, you bitch, she added silently, feeling a surge of hatred which forced the realisation that it had been provoked by jealousy. She hated the thought of Joe and Madeleine together, hated the fact that Joe found Madeleine fascinating, hated having to admit the fact that Madeleine could be fascinating to him. There were layers and layers to Madeleine Kane. The columnist was a complex and extremely clever woman who did not need beauty to draw men to her.

Another waiter passed around dinner menus and Helen pretended to study the itemised list of appetite-teasers. The pain in her heart sent out tortured questions. Why was Joe with Madeleine? He used to hate it when Helen drew other men's attention, yet Madeleine was a mistress at the art of grabbing attention. He certainly did not seem to mind heading that competition. Had he grown so secure that competition no longer worried him? She cast a furtive glance across the table. He was discussing the menu with Madeleine, clearly very much at ease with her.

How had they met? That was the puzzler. An ordinary engineer was not likely to come under the eye of a columnist who wrote about big-name people. The rich and the famous were Madeleine's meat. Where did Joe fit into that scene? But Joe did fit in. He was not looking out of place tonight. It was as if he took such company for granted, an equal among equals.

What had he been doing to change his

circumstances so much? She knew he had gone to America but for how long and for what purpose she had no idea. Joe's mother had been tight-lipped to the point of hostility when Helen had questioned her about him, and that had been all of three years ago. The sense of hopelessness Helen had felt then, evoked a wave of depression which was difficult to push aside even now, when all the evidence confirmed that there never had been any hope of a reconciliation. For all she knew he could have married someone else by now. No, not married, she corrected herself decisively. Madeleine did not play with married men.

The waiter returned and took their orders for dinner. Helen noticed that Joe did not play safe with a simple meal. He ordered the mussels steamed in white wine and the roast duck with cherries, obviously at ease with *haute cuisine* too. She remembered the spaghetti and pasta which were always served at the Torelli table and was even more puzzled.

The waiter collected their menus and retired. Max was in conference with the wine waiter, settling the problem of fitting appropriate wine to the food ordered. Helen suddenly realised that Joe was dominating her thoughts to the exclusion of all else. And she was here with Max. The man she had consented to marry. What Joe did or had done no longer had any relevance to her life and it was stupid to let his presence disturb her so much.

Determination and pride switched on the razzle-dazzle smile which projected vibrant interest as she turned to Jimmy Danvers. 'That was quite a coup you pulled off this morning, trapping the P.M. into an admission of poor judgment.'

Jimmy laughed, delighted with her and himself. 'You haven't heard nuthin' yet!' he crowed. 'Keep tuned! I've got a whole set of politicians lined up for interviews and the punchline for each talk is going to be ... Well, it seemed like a good idea at the time, but ...'

His clever mimic of political sincerity brought a genuine grin from Helen. 'I don't know why they put their heads on your chopping-block, Jimmy.'

He sliced her a sly look. 'If they don't it means they've got something to hide and they know I'll have no compunction in suggesting that to my listeners.'

'The good old power-play,' Helen drawled.

Jimmy winked. 'Got it in one.'

Cheryl leaned forward. 'No one would ever refuse to go on Jimmy's show, Helen. Everyone listens to him,' she declared, her big, brown eyes, dewy with adoration.

Helen almost gagged. Cheryl was probably older than herself but she clung to the role of teenage fan-club cheerleader. There was no attempt at sophistication in the frilly, apple-green, chiffon dress and the frothy mass of coppery curls would have done Shirley Temple

proud. However, Jimmy obviously found no fault
in her. His indulgent smile held unadulterated
pleasure.

But then Jimmy was a prime example of the
male middle-age syndrome. The trendy pattern
Nehru jacket, the gold chains, the over-long, so-
very-carefully-styled hair; all bespoke a grim
hanging on to the 'with-it' image of youth. He
turned back to Helen with an arch look.

'And speaking of tit-bits for my listeners, your
engagement to Max holds some spice.'

'Not at all. Very bread-and-butter,' she
retorted blandly.

But Jimmy was not to be put off and she
answered his questions cautiously, well aware
that he would repeat anything she said, along
with his own titillating interpretations.

A burst of laughter from the Chissolms drew
his attention. All too conscious of Joe sitting next
to them Helen directed her gaze to the vibrant
couple. They were both black-haired and dark-
eyed and they always affected a look-alike image.
Tonight they were dressed in a deep, burgundy-
red, Bart in a brocaded jacket, Penny in sleek
satin. They were sleek people, very polished and
very slick with the tongue. Their faces were
remarkably expressive, eyebrows constantly
emphasising, mouths pursing, pouting, widening.
Their mobile delight was directed at Joe.

'And what is provoking such loud merriment?'
Jimmy demanded.

'Joe has a very dry wit,' Bart informed him.

'He's been describing his difficulties in communication when he was on a lecture tour in the Southern States of America. Had to keep his speech in slow motion.'

Jimmy immediately began relating some amusing anecdotes about different accents and since the focus of the conversation had moved to Joe, Helen could not help speculating about him once more. A lecture tour? It made him sound important. But then he had to hold some importance for Madeleine to find him interesting.

The consultation with the wine waiter finally ended and Max settled back in his chair with an air of complete relaxation. Helen threw him a smile and he lifted his glass in a silent toast to her. For a few moments his gaze was warmly concentrated on her and Helen felt a wave of relief. It was all right. She and Max made a good team. Her abstraction over Joe tonight was only a temporary aberration. It would pass and life would go on. With Max.

His gaze drifted to Madeleine and Helen tensed. She did not want Max to fire another salvo at Madeleine. She did not want to draw Madeleine's hatred again. She breathed more easily as he simply listened and observed. A slight frown creased a V between his eyes. Helen sensed the irritation behind it. He could not place Joe either. But Max had no inhibitions about confronting the situation.

'Joe Torelli,' he drawled, rolling the name off his tongue as though tasting it. He raised an inquiring eyebrow at Madeleine. 'Should I know the name?'

The smile which grew on Madeleine's face held all the feline smugness of a cat who had cornered the cream market. 'It's a name that's already changing the world, Max. Not that you'd know that, since you only deal in flesh,' she added derisively.

'Hardly the world, Madeleine,' Joe remarked.

The green eyes flitted flirtatiously at him. 'That's how my editor described you, darling. Go and get a human interest story on the man, he said, and he meant THE MAN in capital letters.' She turned back to Max, oozing self-satisfaction. 'And I found Joe ve . . . ry human and ve . . . ry interesting.'

'When does your column on Joe come out, Madeleine?' Jimmy Danvers asked interestedly.

'Tomorrow.'

'Tell you what, Joe. How about coming on my radio-programme later this week? I think my listeners would be interested. God knows our lives are becoming more and more ruled by computers. Hate the damned things myself, but you can't get away from them nowadays.'

'I don't think so, thanks, Jimmy,' Joe replied equably. 'For one thing I don't need that kind of publicity, and I find it difficult to talk of my work in layman's language.'

'You talked to Madeleine,' he argued.

Joe grinned. 'Well, Madeleine talked to me in layman's language and she does have a way of getting under a man's skin.'

Jimmy roared with laughter at the pun. Keith joined in and the rest of the table was obviously titillated. Helen swallowed hard, forcing back the bile which had risen to her throat.

Madeleine preened herself. With exaggerated grace she reached out and stroked the strong hand which was curled around a glass. 'And we understood each other very well, didn't we, Joe?'

He lifted the glass in a toast to her. 'But then you are a remarkably understanding woman.'

'Well, much as I admire your smart brain, Joe,' Keith Farrell declared with a hint of chagrin, 'you're going to cost me one hell of a lot of money to update when the time comes.'

'It'll pay,' Joe assured him confidently.

'I'm counting on that.' Keith turned his gaze to Max and smiled. He had a point to score off his old friend. 'You should include the *Scientific Journal* among your girlie magazines, Max. You obviously haven't heard of the Torelli microchip. A miracle of engineering. Going to revolutionise computer technology. The big Americans can't buy it fast enough. How many millions have you squeezed out of them, Joe?'

'Ask my accountants, Keith. Maybe you can get a straight answer from them. I never seem able to,' he answered diffidently.

Keith laughed. 'Ah yes! Cautious men, accountants. But I bet they love you, my friend.'

'Yes. It's easy to love a man with wealth,' Joe remarked and the dark eyes suddenly stabbed

Helen with knife-edge bitterness.

Her reaction was instant and equally bitter. How dare he imply that! She had given him her love when he had barely a cent to call his own. 'Congratulations, Joe,' she said, deliberately holding his taunting gaze before flicking a pointed look at Madeleine. 'You must feel very satisfied with your success.'

'Well, it does have compensations,' he drawled.

Helen put on her best camera smile. 'I'm so glad for you.' Then with the air of having discharged a polite obligation she turned to Max and softened her smile to a more genuine one. 'All the same, I'd rather deal with flesh than machines.'

Max laughed appreciation of her support and when Jimmy Danvers good-humouredly echoed her sentiments and drew Max into conversation about the forthcoming Joel Thomas tour, Helen could retreat behind a mask of pretended interest.

So now she knew what Joe had been doing and all the odd pieces of tonight's jigsaw fell into place. Joe was a man to be reckoned with now, a man of power and wealth. He had left his student days long behind. And he had left Nell Daley long behind. He could pick and choose any woman he liked, confident that he could keep her interest, maybe even careless of whether he kept her interest or not. The contempt he had shown Helen tonight certainly indicated such an attitude.

She remembered the passionate avowals of

love, the agonising desperation in those final hours, the wild heights and painful lows of their relationship. Could such strong emotion be forgotten? Had he dismissed it all from his mind, just as he had dismissed her from his life? She lifted her long lashes and looked at him, searching for answers.

He was laughing with Penny Chissolm. His gaze swung slowly around and caught Helen's scrutiny. For one ungarded moment there was a look which caught at her heart, squeezed it unmercifully. The sad hollowness of that final parting pulsed between them, that dreadful moment when all the cruel, hateful words had been said and their love had been torn in too many tatters to be recovered.

Then his gaze dropped. Her skin scorched with shame as the dark eyes followed the V-neckline of her dress, pausing at the soft swell of breasts so blatantly revealed by the low cleavage. She could hear the words as though he had spoken them out loud. 'Flaunting your body to get every man hot for you.' She had not been guilty of it then. It had all been in Joe's mind.

He turned back to Madeleine.

Helen wanted to scream at him, tell him it wasn't true, but the dress condemned her. The scream faded into a wretched plea which died into a silent whimper of pain. There was nothing she could do or say. It was all over long ago, and it had all been said and done.

CHAPTER THREE

THE entrées arrived. Helen prodded at the warm avocado salad, her stomach churning far too much to digest even the blandest food. Damn, damn, damn Joe! she cursed, more from irritation with herself than with venom towards him. He shouldn't be able to make her feel guilty, not after all these years.

There was no reason to feel ashamed of her body. Or the dress she wore. As Max would say; if you've got it, flaunt it! No profit in hiding your light under a bushel! Max loved her body ... well, desired it anyway. He never criticised, never put her down, never made her feel guilty about anything. He liked her just as she was. And that made her feel good.

She took a defiant sip of Chablis. Louis-Latour. One of the best white wines of France, Max declared. Rich, golden, full-bodied. It slid down her throat as smooth as silk. She drank some more. To hell with Joe! At least her marriage to Max promised to be a fair exchange, two people respecting each other's abilities, not master and slave. With her stomach more settled she forked into the salad and ate it with no trouble at all. The Chablis washed it down. It really was a great wine.

The entrée plates were cleared away and the war between Max and Madeleine resumed. It was waged under a cover of civility, a certain playfulness, clever repartee, laughter, but every word and move was calculated for its effectiveness as a weapon. Joe readily allied himself to Madeleine's play and as a matter of pride, Helen followed Max's lead, using every bit of sophistication she had ever learnt. She did not like this malicious cat-and-mouse game but she was determined to show Joe that she was as free of him as he was of her. And the wine helped dull her sensibilities.

The main course arrived. The '53 Lafite was proudly poured. Max burbled on about its qualities. Keith signalled a waiter and sat back smugly as a '45 Mouton was brought in, a special present for Max's birthday. The party became a little livelier. Speeches were tossed off between eating and drinking. Helen's rack of lamb was beautifully tender, the accompanying vegetables superbly cooked. And the wine was very, very good.

Helen was beginning to feel exceedingly mellow by the time the meal was over. She sat back and inadvertently glanced across at Madeleine. Green-eyed venom looked back at her. Helen sucked in her breath and looked away. The wine had not mellowed Madeleine. Helen had never been the target for such undiluted hatred. She did not understand it and at the moment her brain was too fuzzy to come to grips with it.

The main course was cleared from the table and platters of cheese set down. The orchestra began playing another bracket of numbers. Apparently Keith Farrell's attention had been flagging. Jill Amory stood, swung her long mane of ash-blonde hair over her shoulders and began swaying to the beat of the music. Her white dress was a loose sheath, draped from a glittering clasp on one shoulder. The sinuous movement of curves under the soft, clinging material was a provocative invitation.

'Come on, Keith. You've sat there long enough. I want to dance.'

He groaned. She pouted and moved closer, thrusting a hip at him as she turned her back to the rest of the company. Her husky voice was pitched too low for words to be distinct but whatever she said got results. Keith's grin was pure lechery. He slapped her on the rump and climbed to his feet, directing a smug wink at the rest of them.

'I guess it's as good an excuse as any to feel a woman's fanny,' he rumbled crudely.

Helen winced. Keith Farrell's attitude to women always grated on her. She wondered how Jill Amory could stand him but all the evidence suggested that she could, and no doubt she was profiting by the association. That was a mean thought, Helen chided herself. Who was she to judge? She did not love Max. But there was more to their relationship than sex. They had not even had sex. Yet. Sex without love . . .

'Good idea!' Max suddenly declared, and his grin reflected Keith's as he bent towards her. 'Shall we dance, my love? I have an irresistible urge to hold you in my arms. The food was good, the wine superb, and all I need is thou.'

The desire in his eyes and the seductive softness of his voice provoked an unco-ordinated reaction from Madeleine. She turned away too abruptly and her hand knocked a glass. Joe caught it as it tipped. Having righted the glass he stood before Max had risen to his feet.

'Let's show them what it is to dance, Madeleine,' he invited smoothly.

So all four of them went out on deck. It was a beautiful night, just as the Head Waiter had predicted. Only the lightest of breezes feathered Helen's skin. The night sky was studded with so many stars it was like a continuation of the city lights. There were several couples dancing, others leaning against the railing, enjoying the fresh air. Helen noticed Keith Farrell's large hands clutching Jill Amory's bottom and could not help a grimace of disgust. Joe and Madeleine moved into a clinch. Helen turned into Max's arms and closed her eyes. The fresh air had made her feel quite ill all of a sudden.

Max pressed her close, making every movement a sensual exercise, thighs brushing thighs to the throb of the music. One hand roved over her bare back, caressing her skin to sensitivity. His mouth brushed against her hair. Despite his declared desire, he was not sexually aroused. And neither was Helen. To her horror she felt nothing, not the slightest pin-prick of excitement. Max's body emanated warmth but there was a dreadful chill invading her veins.

Tonight Max would expect to share her bed. What if she could not respond to him? This afternoon, tonight, right up to the moment she saw Joe, Helen was confident that there would at least be sexual fulfilment in their relationship. Now she was not at all sure. This unlooked-for meeting with Joe had to be affecting her too deeply. And Max was not helping. His attention was not really focussed on her. The contest of wits with Madeleine had been consuming him all night. He was going through the motions but his body was simply following a formula.

Yet nothing had really changed. Helen had not pretended to herself that she loved Max and Max had certainly not pretended that he loved her. The advantages in their proposed marriage were still the same. There was no reason to change her mind.

Except that she still loved Joe. The thought slid into her fuzzy brain and much as she tried to reject it, there was no rejecting its truth. The scars he had left on her heart had been pulsing all night.

The music stopped. Max did not loosen his embrace. His hand reached under her hair and held the nape of her neck. 'Helen...' he whispered huskily.

Reluctantly she lifted her head, knowing he wanted to kiss her. She watched his mouth coming closer to hers and waited passively for the contact. Maybe it would awaken some spark of response.

'Max!' Madeleine's voice was sharp with unguarded emotion.

'Mmmh?' It was a hum of preoccupation yet it ended on an expectant note. Max had obviously been aware of Madeleine's approach.

The orchestra struck up another number.

'I have a fancy to dance with you, Max.' The tone had changed to a cajoling purr. 'It is your birthday, darling, and I seem to remember we danced together ten years ago. I've forgotten if you were any good.'

'Then I shall remind you . . .' he purred back, '. . . if Helen doesn't object,' he added, emphasising that Helen came first with him.

'Oh, I can recommend Joe. He's a marvellous dancer. I'm sure Helen won't mind a whirl around the deck with him,' Madeleine drawled as she insinuated her arm between them and drew Max aside.

She was left facing Joe. Neither one of them made a move to dance. All the nerves in Helen's body had sprung into jangling life. She did not want Joe to touch her, could not bear the thought of being in his arms when those arms no longer held her with love. He was Madeleine's lover now. Her head spun with the conflict of wanting him, yet feeling repelled.

'It's been a long time,' he said softly, so softly the words were barely audible.

'Yes,' she whispered, not trusting herself to meet his eyes, too frightened of revealing how vulnerable she felt. She forced a little more volume into her voice. 'Would you excuse me please, Joe? I think I've drunk too much wine. I really should go back to the dining-room and sit down.'

'Won't you dance with me this once, Nell?'

She had already turned away in her anxiety to escape the situation. His voice floated over her shoulder, trapping her into stillness. Her heart thumped its warning of his power to drain her will. For a long time Joe had had only to ask and Helen would have given him anything. But that time was past.

It angered her to find herself vulnerable to a soft request. He had been cruel, even contemptuous towards her at the table, showing a sublime indifference to anything she might feel. How dare he now pluck at the strings which he had severed? It had to be a mere whim. A test to see if he still held any power over her heart. Male ego. Well, let him eat his own words and find satisfaction in them.

'I didn't think you'd want to dance with Helen of Troy, Joe,' she muttered bitterly.

There was a sharply indrawn breath. 'Oh, Christ!' The oath hissed out, carrying a deep, wrenching frustration. Another indrawn breath, then words dragged from stifled pain. 'Nell . . . I am sorry for that stupid crack. I don't know why . . .' He sighed. 'Goddamnit! I didn't come here tonight with any wish to hurt you. But when . . .' Again he sighed. 'Nell, please . . . I would like . . . very much . . . to have one last dance with you.'

She turned, irresistibly drawn by a plea which had ripped through her brittle defences. Still she hesitated, driven by her own pain to question the need in his voice. 'You didn't act as if you cared.'

His eyes glittered down at her revealing a deep yearning which struck the same chord in her own soul.

'How could I not care?' The words were a throb of barely suppressed passion. 'From the moment I first met you I've been obsessed with you.' The slight shake of his head seemed to be an attempt to negate the feeling but it was still in his eyes when he spoke again and the curl of his mouth mocked himself. 'How could I not care, Nell?'

She felt so confused that she was hardly aware of being drawn towards him. Then she did not have the will to stop the action. He cradled her in his arms with a tenderness which almost moved her to tears, so reminiscent was it of their very first embrace so long ago.

Their bodies touched. Instantly the old chemistry tingled into dangerous life. His hands slid over the nakedness of her back and she shuddered so violently that a pretence of indifference was impossible. His hold on her tightened. She felt his chest expand and a long breath wavered through her hair.

His hard, muscular thighs forced her legs into a rhythmic sequence of dance-steps. She moved stiffly, conscious of a wave of heat surging through her veins. She was suddenly very frightened of giving in to that heat and melting into the body which called so strongly to hers. She could not afford to do that. It would be a betrayal of herself and of the commitment she had given to Max. She strained away, trying to put a little distance between them and thereby lessen the temptation.

Joe pressed her closer. Strong fingers entwined themselves in the silk of her hair and gently urged her head on to his shoulder. The resistance she had tried to muster collapsed with full body contact. It had been so long . . . so long . . . and she had never wanted anyone but Joe.

Her heart beat a wild protest at the violence being done to it. A thousand memories were rampant, coursing through every part of her, filling her mind and awakening responses which shamed her. Tears pricked her eyes, a wash of despair at her complete lack of control.

'Remember how it was with us . . . the good times, Nell.'

The soft whisper seduced her further into the past, recalling all too poignantly the love they had shared; the joy of being together, talking, touching, belonging. But the other memories came too and they could not be forgotten. The scars went too deep.

'Do you love him?'

The tight little murmur rasped in her ear and pricked at the old wounds. Joe had no right to ask. He had thrown aside any right to ask when he had thrown away her love. Her body might be weak but her mind was very strong on that point.

'Nell?'

His persistence brought pain and she retaliated with the bitterness he had taught her. 'Love didn't work very well for us, Joe.'

There was a momentary stiffening, a hesitation before his feet picked up the beat again. She had scored a hit. The thought slid into her mind with such malicious satisfaction that Helen was shocked at herself.

With one intuitive leap she understood the feeling between Max and Madeleine. They had loved once, and whatever had rotted their love had left festering sores which compelled them to hit out and hurt. Love and hatred, two sides of the one coin. Helen sighed, painfully aware of the tug-of-war in her own heart.

'Then you don't love him.'

The taut statement grated on her but she resisted the impulse to answer sharply. She forced her voice to a steady neutral. 'I can live with Max.'

He stopped dancing. 'I was right,' he muttered grimly and then his hands were on her upper arms, pushing her away so that he could look down at her face, his eyes burning with a feverish urgency. 'All those things you want, wealth, status, beautiful things . . . I can give them to you now. Anything at all. I can match Max at buying whatever you want. I can take you wherever you want to go. I'm at least his equal. So don't marry him, Nell. Marry me. You'll not only have everything you crave for but love too, because I love you, Nell, and he doesn't. He doesn't.'

Her anger had grown with each assertion he had made. Blind! He had always been blinded by pride. His total lack of perception was so offensive she could hardly speak. 'You think Max is buying me with those things,' she bit out scathingly.

Doubt flickered across his eyes but the rage in Helen gave him no time to retract.

'Trust and respect!' she hammered at him with all the vehemence of old resentments. 'That's what he's giving me, Joe. They can't be bought. I'm good at my job and Max is giving me a partnership. He's prepared to accept what I can give. He actually wants what I can give. He values what I can give. Are you getting the message, Joe? What I . . . I can give. Max doesn't see me as a doll he has to take out and entertain. He sees me as a person he can share his life with. Sharing everything. Equals. And that's why I'm marrying him.'

She wrenched herself out of Joe's grasp and strode away from him, tears of anger and frustration burning her eyes. She was about to re-enter the dining-room when a hand clutched her elbow and she found herself being forcibly steered down the deck to the rear of the ferry.

'Let me go!' she hissed at him.

Joe's hold remained relentlessly firm. 'Not until we've talked this out.'

'You have no right . . .'

'At this moment I don't give a damn about rights!'

The deck had narrowed. Joe pushed her past the kitchen area, around the corner to the darkness of the small rear deck. He almost flung her against the wall and imprisoned her there with one arm on either side of her. His face was working with violent emotion. He bent his head and sucked in a deep breath.

'Now, let's have the truth!'

CHAPTER FOUR

'IF all you wanted was trust and respect, why the hell did you enter that Goddamned beauty contest?'

Helen's mind reeled back into the past. The hard accusation in Joe's eyes, the bitter contempt in his voice, the fierce aggression emanating from his body . . . it was that dreadful night all over again. And just as then, Joe did not wait for an answer.

'I told you how I felt about it. What trust could you expect when you sneaked into it behind my back? As for respect, what self-respecting woman would take part in a meat parade?'

She was trembling. Helen sucked in a deep breath to steady herself. She did not have to take this abuse. It was not four years ago and Joe's opinion of her shouldn't matter. Ignoring the pain in her heart, she spoke with quiet precision.

'You don't want the truth, Joe. You've got your mind all made up on me. You're no more ready to listen now than you were when it really mattered. So let me go.'

He bent his head, shaking it from side to side. 'It matters. It still matters,' he bit out with harsh emphasis, and when he lifted his head his eyes burnt into hers with compelling intensity. 'Why, Nell? Tell me why!'

Without asking herself why she should respond, driven by a need to set the record straight, Helen dredged through her memory for the exact truth. 'I think . . . because . . . you disapproved of it so much . . .'

Joe snorted in disbelief. 'Oh, come on, Nell! That makes no sense at all. You went in it for what you could get out of it. The clothes, the car, the trip overseas, the fame and fortune . . . everything that I couldn't give you.'

His cutting derision opened the old wounds and out poured the bitter resentments which had festered under Joe's pride. 'Yes! I wanted them!' she snapped at him. 'But not just for me. For us! I wanted you to accept what I could bring to our relationship. Your disapproval made no sense to me. Why shouldn't we have had a car if I was lucky enough to win a prize?'

The choked feeling which had grown under his criticisms in the old days came back to her, tightening her voice. 'You were always putting me down, especially over anything to do with modelling, even though you knew I took those jobs to support myself. I wanted to show you that you shouldn't disapprove. That it could be worth something to us.'

'Oh, great!' he mocked. 'It was going to do our relationship a lot of good with me stuck at home and you tripping overseas for a year. I can just see you coming back to good old Joe after you'd tasted the good life, the glamour and the star treatment all over the whole damned world. Do you actually believe that you would've come back and been content with me, a poor engineer struggling to get on in the world?'

The scornful stab of his voice ruptured the bitter defence she had hurled at him. The emotional desolation of four long years gushed through, swallowing up the aggression. Tears welled into her eyes and she had no strength or will to stop them.

'I did come back.' There was no fight, no resentment in the words. They were the dull echo of despair. 'I needed you so much I would've crawled on my hands and knees to you, begging you to take me back and love me.' The tears spilled over and coursed down her cheeks and her voice choked into sobs. 'But you weren't there. You'd gone to America. And your mother couldn't . . . or wouldn't . . . give me an address. So I went on living without you.'

He closed his eyes as the blood drained from his face, leaving it stark white in the moonlight. 'Oh, no! No! Oh, Christ!' The agonised mutter was barely audible. His arms dropped away from the wall. He turned and almost reeled over to the railing. His hands clutched it tightly as he swayed back and forth like someone trying to contain unbearable grief. When he finally spoke, the words dragged out. 'I didn't know . . . I didn't know . . . she didn't tell me.'

'I loved you, Joe,' she threw at him from a

crest of billowing pain. 'Why couldn't you believe me? I didn't want to go away. I just wanted you to accept me.' Her head rolled from side to side against the wall as if buffeted by the memories which poured from her mouth in a stream of uncontrollable anguish.

'I was so frightened when I won that contest. I'd only gone into it out of some crazy sense of rebellion. And then suddenly it was real, and more than I'd bargained for. I told the organisers that I didn't want the winner's contract. To give it to the runner-up. They insisted that I think about it overnight. But you wouldn't listen. You wouldn't listen, Joe. You told me to go. And I felt so lost. So totally rejected. So I went where I thought I was wanted. But it was wrong. It wasn't what I wanted. It never was. Never. But you wouldn't believe me. And I didn't care what I did after you ... after you called me a whore and ...'

'Don't!' The cry was sharp with pain. He swung around, his face a tortured mask. 'I had to end it. I couldn't take any more.'

'Take what?' she choked out in painful bewilderment.

'Oh, Nell ... Nell ...' The name was a groan of need as he came to her, cupping her face with reverent hands, his eyes drinking in the perfection of her features with a yearning which was almost idolatry. 'You're so beautiful. Don't you see? You're a rich man's woman. Max called you unique and that's what you are ... like a unique piece of art. And you'll always be coveted by men who want the best. How could I compete? A poor student with nothing to his name. You were my whole world but I knew I wasn't yours . . .'

'You were,' she insisted, emotion furring her voice. 'You didn't have to compete. There was no competition. I never wanted any other man but you.'

His eyes held bitter self-mockery. 'Only because I made damned sure you weren't in their company long enough. But in my heart I knew there was always going to be a bigger world for you, Nell. It was there waiting for you all the time. If you'd stayed with me, how long do you think a marriage between us would have lasted when you and I would both have known that there were so many better things for you, if you so willed it?'

'No. No!' she denied vehemently.

'Nell, your eyes were continually drawn to them. You'd come back from your modelling jobs and describe the lovely, fascinating clothes that you'd worn. And the celebrities you'd met. I hated hearing about them.' His grimace was full of self-disgust. 'I tried to take away your pleasure in those things because I was scared they'd take you away from me. It was wrong and it was selfish and I knew it. I didn't like the person I was turning into any more than you did. But I couldn't help myself, Nell.'

He sighed and shook his head. 'When you talked about that damned beauty contest, all I could think of was stopping you, because I knew you'd win. You couldn't miss. And then the world you wanted would be at your feet and I couldn't be part of it.'

'I didn't want the world. I didn't,' she pleaded brokenly, tears gathering again at the memory of that disastrous night. 'Only the world we could make together. I just wanted you to accept that I could help. It was the wrong way, going in that beauty contest, but somehow it summed up all the things you disapproved about me, and if I won a prize I was going to say . . . see? It means nothing except an advantage to us. You and me, Joe.' The tears spilled over and she bent her head in uncontrollable distress. 'Just you and me,' she sobbed.

'Don't cry! Don't cry!' The harsh rasp was half-muffled in her hair as he wrapped his arms around her and rocked her in a fierce embrace. 'We're together now if you can forgive me. Those things I said to you that night. I didn't mean them, Nell. I was dying inside and I lashed out, wanting to hurt as I was hurting. And all the time I wanted you so badly it was gnawing my guts out. I've never stopped wanting you. Always you, Nell. Only you.'

His mouth grazed over her hair, pressing a trail of feverish kisses and the raw need in him vibrated through her body and echoed around the four-year-old emptiness which had been waiting for love to fill. It ignited the need which had been smouldering from the first moment of seeing Joe and there was no smothering it. The barriers were down and Helen was helpless to deny either of them.

Her hands curled around his neck, wanting, needing to hold on to him. Her face tilted upwards, lips slightly parted, inviting, yearning for the love which had been theirs. Joe's mouth closed over hers and the passion for possession surged between them, compelling in its demand to be satisfied. Again and again they kissed, driven to give and take, to own, to share, to be swallowed up in a togetherness which could never be sundered.

Their bodies strained for closer intimacy. Joe pressed Helen hard against the unyielding support of the wall behind her, and she revelled in the firmer contact, relearning the sensual excitement of arousal. And she wanted it all. Her fingers raced to undo Joe's coat-button. She slid her hands over his silk shirt, around the lean waist and up over the rippling muscles of his back in an ecstasy of ownership. This was Joe. Joe whom she loved and who loved her.

He rained kisses all over her face and she turned it this way and that for his worship, capturing every imprint of his need for her, elation bubbling over the heat of desire which pounded through her veins, drumming everything else out of existence.

Joe unfastened the halter around her neck and lovingly caressed the silk away from her breasts. 'You're so beautiful, Nell . . . so beautiful . . .'

The husky murmur was sweet to her ears, as sweet as the caress of his hands on her flesh. Dear God! How she had ached for his touch all these years! And the ripples of pleasure grew in strength, swelling to an urgent tide of desire which was beyond her will to control.

A motor-boat churned past. A loud wolf-whistle rent the spell of their intimacy. Instinctively protective, Joe hugged Helen close to cover her semi-nakedness with his body but his warmth was no counter to the sudden chill of reality. The heat of desire which had melted all sense of time and place was quick-frozen in Helen's veins. Her eyes opened wide with horror.

It was all a dream. A step-back in time. Joe was not hers. He had come here with Madeleine. Madeleine Kane. And she had committed herself to marrying Max. She shivered, appalled at the weakness which had so nearly led her to a complete betrayal of her word.

Joe misunderstood her sudden tension. 'It's all right,' he murmured, beginning to caress her again. His mouth moved warmly over her temples. 'Nothing matters but this.'

'No! No!' she repeated in growing panic before his touch could seduce her reason again. She pushed him away and scrabbled for her halter top with trembling hands. 'You shouldn't have done this. I shouldn't have let you. You can't cut out four years and pretend we're back there.'

'I'm not pretending. We're here and now. I love you, Nell, and you love me,' Joe insisted passionately, his hands taking possession of her waist as Helen fastened her top and agitatedly smoothed it around her breasts, breasts which were still tingling with sensitivity. 'We can have our life together, starting tonight,' Joe declared.

Her eyes flared up at him, wounded and proud. 'No! This is madness! You destroyed me once and you never even bothered to look me up and see if anything had survived. Anytime in the last four years you could have come to me. But you didn't, Joe. And tonight is too late. Tonight I promised to marry Max. You're just too damned late, Joe.'

His fingers dug into her flesh. 'You can't marry him now. You love me.'

She stared up at Joe, her heart pounding an instinctive response to him. But did she love him? She had loved him, but what did she know of him now? Four years and not a word from him. A lot had happened in those four years. Hadn't she seen the changes in him at the table tonight? And he had come with Madeleine.

'We've been feeding on memories,' she muttered despairingly.

'No! It's the same as it ever was,' he insisted.

But Helen was seeing Madeleine's red fingernails stroking him and her heart suddenly cringed with revulsion. 'Get your hands off me! Get them off!' She cried, plucking frantically at the offensive grasp on her waist.

He removed his hands, only to lift them in urgent appeal. 'Nell, please . . .'

'You're Madeleine's lover!' she spat at him.

'No!'

'Don't lie to me. You made it obvious to everyone at the table.'

She shrank away from him and stepped over to the railing, gulping in the cool, fresh air in the hope it would clear the insanity of re-living the past. She was disgusted with Joe and even more disgusted with herself. How could she have abandoned herself to his lovemaking so ... so mindlessly?

Shame and guilt crawled around her mind, shame that she could still be so vulnerable to Joe when he had ignored her for so many years, and guilt that she had forgotten her commitment to Max, even for a minute. She had been knocked off balance by Joe's sudden re-entrance in her life. Thrown further off balance by the re-hashing of the traumatic end to their love affair.

But now it was necessary for her to think very clearly and not be blinded by an emotion she could not trust. The barren loneliness of four years clamped around her heart, keeping her feeling for Joe at bay. Max had made that loneliness easier to bear this last year and she owed him loyalty if nothing else.

A featherlight touch caressed her bare back. She shuddered. The hand brushed up to her shoulder and gently squeezed despite her flinching reaction.

'Nell, please don't turn away from me.' The voice was persuasively soft.

'You turned me away.' That bitter truth lent an unrelenting ring to her reply.

'Not because I wanted to.'

Helen compressed her lips. They had been through this. It did not explain why he had never tried to contact her. She was pricklingly aware of Joe's nearness but she held herself stiffly in control, determined not to weaken again.

'I can't trust you, Joe. You've hurt me so badly I don't think I can ever forget. And you're here tonight with that woman.'

He sighed and spoke in a flat monotone. 'Madeleine means nothing to me. We haven't been lovers. She issued the invitation to this party when she interviewed me for her column. She said she wanted to show me off to her friends. She dropped Keith's name, then Jimmy's and Max's. I knew you worked with Max. I asked for more details and learnt that you'd be here too. You were the only reason I came with her, Nell. I wanted to see you.'

Again he sighed. 'I pretended to myself that it was just idle curiosity, that you meant nothing to me any more. But one look at you and I knew I'd been kidding myself. Then Max delivered his announcement of your engagement and I felt I'd been punched in the gut. What was there to do after that but support Madeleine? She was hurting badly. And so was I. I played along with her from a sense of pride or self-defence ... I don't know. It made the situation easier to bear. But it meant nothing. You're the only woman who means anything to me, Nell. I love you. I always have. I always will.'

His hand slid to the curve of neck and shoulder and his thumb teased the sensitive spot on her nape. Helen's pulse was leaping erratically, jagging between wild hope and tearing doubt. She wanted to believe him and her body ached to give in to the warmth he was so knowingly provoking.

But reason spread its cold fingers through her brain and pushed out the insidious potency of those sweetly-drugging words. She jerked away in savage recoil from his touch, then swung on him, spitting out her anger.

'What kind of a gullible fool do you take me for, Joe? Oh, you love me so much you didn't bother looking me up. Not once in four years. And by your own admission you're only here tonight because of a chance invitation. Which you accepted out of idle curiosity.'

Scorn poured from the pain in her heart. 'One look at me! What did you feel, Joe? Love or lust! Oh, I'm dressed for the part tonight, aren't I? A high-priced whore! And you're such a big man now. You can afford me. Just offer the highest price. Only it just so happens that Max likes me dressed like this and I did it to please him. Not for you. Or any other man. And I'm not for sale. I never have been and I never will be. And if you think you can get around that little miscalculation by claiming love, you're a little too late to be credible. I will not be picked up like an old shoe and worn at your convenience.'

Her mouth curled in self-derision. 'My God! All these years I've grieved for what we had together, and I bet you haven't even given me a thought. So what is your love worth, Joe?'

'It's worth something to you if you grieved for it,' he replied strongly. 'And you misunderstand me. There was a time I worked eighteen hours a day just to keep the thought of you pushed to the back of my mind. And hope I'd be exhausted enough to sleep without dreaming of you. And eventually I did manage it. You actually did me a favour. If I hadn't obsessed myself with work to forget you, I wouldn't be here tonight.'

His chin lifted aggressively and his voice rang with pride. 'I am a big man now. In my field. I'm one of the best in the world. And it feels a damned sight better than being a poor student who couldn't afford to give his woman what she wanted. When I knew that I'd made it, that all the money I could ever use would come rolling in, I thought of you, Nell. I thought, now I can ask her to marry me.'

'So why didn't you? Why didn't you?' she cried accusingly.

His tone turned to bitterness. 'It was only then that I realised that what I wanted could never be recaptured. If you didn't love me enough to stay with me when I was poor, then all my wealth couldn't buy the love I wanted from you. So I stayed away. And I was right. You're prepared to marry a man you don't love for what he can give you.'

'That's not true!' she defended hotly. 'It's not the money.'

Joe made a sharp, dismissive gesture. 'Position, power, call it what you like. It's not for love, Nell.'

'If that's what you think of me, why do you want to buy me now?' she flung back at him.

His control snapped. His face worked with violent passion as words seethed off his tongue. 'Because that doesn't stop me from loving you. I had only to see you again and I didn't care about anything else. I wanted you as my wife. Marry me, Nell. The feeling is still there for you as well as me.'

Her heart begged her to say yes even as her mind told her it would be no good. Joe took the step which closed the gap between them, his hands sliding around her waist before she could think to evade him. She reached out and clutched the railing, her fingernails digging into the paint in an instinctive need to hold on to reality. Her other hand pressed against his chest as she fought to deny the physical attraction he could still exert.

'Don't use force again, Joe,' she warned bitterly. 'It won't work for you this time.'

His hold tightened, then relaxed, but he did not let her go, his strong will fighting hers all the way. 'I love you, Nell. I love you so much I'd do anything for you.'

She shook her head and tears filmed her eyes, lending a poignant sheen to her inner grief.

'You'll never believe me, will you? You'll always think it's because of what you can do for me. Buying me with your wealth. Lots of men have offered me anything I want, Joe. But I can earn anything I want as far as material goods go. What I really want is to love and be loved. But you'll never believe that.'

'If love is what you want, you won't get it from Max,' he insisted vehemently.

'No. But I might be happy with him. I know I won't be happy with you, Joe.' The tears trickled down her cheeks and she had to force words past the huge lump in her throat. 'You make me feel like a whore. You were right the first time. You can't go back and recapture what we had. It's lost.'

'No!' He shook his head in agonised denial. 'No, I can't let you go! We can make it work this time.' He pulled her hard against him, pinning her there with possessive arms and using his body to impress his words on her. 'We belong together, Nell.'

'Stop it! Let me go!' She cried in anguish, her hands beating at him for release. 'You wouldn't even be here but for Madeleine. You weren't ever going to come back to me. So let it be. Let it be.'

'Nell, please listen to me . . .'

'No more! No more!'

She tore herself out of his grasp and stumbled around the corner before Joe could detain her.

'Wait, Nell!'

A few metres along the deck a man was leaning

against the railing, his face in shadow. The smoke from a cigar curled around his head. Helen walked quickly towards him, half-blinded by tears and intent on denying Joe another private *tête-à-tête*. Her wrist was caught from behind just as she drew level with the man.

'No!' she hissed over her shoulder.

The man straightened and turned around.

'I think you've had a fair enough innings, Joe,' Max drawled. 'Helen, will you join me in a breath of fresh air?' He stretched out a hand in invitation.

'No!' Joe's voice in her ear, low and passionate, hands on her waist, holding her back. 'Listen to me, Nell. Give me the chance to prove that you're wrong about me. Don't commit yourself to him. Wait and see.'

Her heart ached for the promise in Joe's words. But she had waited ... and waited ... and waited. And now she had seen that it really was gone, that magical love which had existed before misunderstandings had undermined it. She could not bear any more emotional torture. It was ripping her apart, just as it had done in the past.

Max's hand remained outstretched. His gaze held hers steadily, neither demanding nor retreating, letting her make her own decision without persuasion of any kind. She lifted her hand.

'He doesn't love you.' The fierce protest from Joe was a hiss of entreaty.

'Neither do you, Joe,' Helen said with sad

finality and placed her hand in Max's. 'If you
love me, the kindest thing you can do for me is to
let me go and stay out of my life, just as you
planned to do all along.'

'No!'

'Helen has made her choice, Joe. I believe
you'll find Madeleine back at the table,' Max said
pointedly.

Joe's hands dropped away. Max drew Helen to
his side. Joe did not leave. He did not move. For
several, long moments he stared down at their
linked hands. Slowly, so slowly he raised his eyes
and gave Helen a look which accused her of
betrayal. 'He is buying you, Nell. In his own
way. He doesn't love you and you don't love
him.'

Helen shook her head, weary of the torment.
'No. You're the one who thinks he can buy. You
make everything so ugly, Joe. Please go.'

A look of sheer agony passed over his face,
leaving it drawn and pale. 'I do love you, Nell,'
he said in a voice which rasped with choking
emotion. 'I'll always love you. I'm sorry for the
pain I've given you. I'll go away if that's what
you want. I hope Max can give you ... the
happiness ... that I ... that I destroyed.'

Then he turned like a drunken man and walked
away.

CHAPTER FIVE

WAS she wrong? Dear God! Could she be wrong? No, no, no. Joe's obsession with her was not love. Not the kind of all-sharing, understanding love she wanted. But that look in his eyes ... the accusation and despair ... had cut straight to her heart. She shivered.

Max slid an arm around her shoulders and tucked her comfortingly against him. 'Would you rather go back inside?' he asked softly.

She shook her head. He turned them both so that they could lean against the railing, letting the night enclose them in privacy.

'Want my coat?'

'No. No, thank-you.' She sucked in a steadying breath. 'I'm not really cold. Just reaction, I guess. I'm sorry, Max,' she muttered self-consciously. 'It was ...'

'Nothing to apologise for. I saw him walk you down the deck and you're not the type to make a scene, Helen. One of the things I admire about you, that innate dignity which carries you through any upset.' He puffed on his cigar and slowly exhaled the smoke, idly watching it as it dissipated in the light breeze.

Max would not think her so dignified if he had seen her abandoned response to Joe, Helen thought in silent shame.

'Rough meeting,' he murmured, more as a comment than a question.

Impossible to pretend innocence. 'We were lovers once,' she said bluntly.

Max threw her a wry little smile. 'That figured. It was seeing him that shocked you when we came on board, wasn't it?'

'Yes.'

He nodded and dropped his gaze to the water, watching it for a while before looking out at the harbourside lights. 'He didn't look at you enough. A man might not go after a beautiful woman but he looks at her. The omission was too deliberate. He wants you very badly.' He drew on his cigar before adding softly, 'Do you want him, Helen?'

The question hit her hard. 'I . . . no . . . no, it's in the past,' she answered, reason once more overriding the clamour of her heart.

He quirked an eyebrow at her. 'You wouldn't be saying that out of some idiotic sense of integrity, would you? I won't rant and rave if you want to change your mind about marrying me. It's your life, my dear.'

Her cheeks burnt with guilt. She had not given Max a thought while Joe was making love to her. Love and desire had overwhelmed common sense and there was no point in pretending it hadn't happened. 'Max, I don't know any more. I feel . . . I feel pretty shaken up at the moment.'

He nodded, and unexpectedly there was

compassion in his eyes. It spurred Helen to be direct with him.

'What about you?' she asked, unsure of how he viewed the situation as it now stood. 'Do you still want to marry me?'

'Why not? Nothing's changed for me,' he answered equably.

'I thought ... maybe ...' She stopped, too tongue-tied with embarrassment to go on.

'Because Joe was your lover?' he finished for her with dry amusement. 'My darling girl, I am hardly lily-white.' He eyed her curiously for a moment, then added, 'Don't tell me he's been the only one.'

She nodded.

His breath was expelled in a low whistle. 'Four years! What a wicked waste of time!'

The remark provoked a wry smile from Helen. 'Probably. I don't have your cavalier attitude to sex, Max. I just never felt like ... felt strongly enough about anyone else.' She sighed and there was a wealth of sadness in the sound.

Again Max eyed her curiously but there was more serious speculation in his eyes this time. 'What about me, Helen? Do I turn you on? That is rather critical, you know.'

She hesitated, honesty forcing her to give a qualified answer. 'You did earlier tonight.'

'Before you met Joe,' he added quietly.

Shame brought a scorching heat to her cheeks as that scene on the rear-deck burnt across her mind. She had been turned on all right. Almost to the point of no return.

Max brushed her cheek with cool fingertips. 'I wouldn't want you pretending I'm Joe, Helen. It wouldn't work.'

She met his questioning gaze with bleak candour. 'I don't want to pretend you're Joe.' She hesitated, but Joe's accusation was still scraping raw wounds. 'Max, do you think you're buying me?'

One eyebrow rose in sardonic amusement. 'Helen, I've worked with you too long not to know you're a woman of integrity. I think you accepted me for the same reason I asked you. We both need something more in our lives. Call it a need for companionship if you like. Someone who's always there.'

'Then . . .' Some demon inside her insisted that Max deny any obsession with her beauty. 'Max, I know you get a kick out of others' reaction to my . . .' Her tongue gagged on the word, beauty. ' . . . my appearance, but that's not why you want to marry me, is it? You don't regard me as a . . . as a piece of art you want to own?'

'Madeleine thinks so.' He gave a short derisive laugh which ended in a grimace. 'Beauty is a much over-rated item where marriage is concerned. Caroline taught me that lesson in no time flat.' He shook his head. 'No, my dear. I wouldn't marry you if that was all you had to offer me.'

The hand he had lifted to her face cupped her cheek and his thumb lightly stroked the fine skin as he spoke. 'I enjoy the fact that you're beautiful. I expect to get a great deal of visual and sensual pleasure from having you as my wife. But what I like most is being able to talk to you. You immediately catch on to what I'm saying and your response invariably gives me satisfaction. That's what makes us a good team.' He dropped his hand and shrugged. 'I think it's the crux of a good marriage . . . communication.'

Yes. Communication. If there had bëen more communication between Joe and her in the old days . . . oh, give it away, she told herself tiredly. Leave the agony in the past.

'Joe still gets to you, doesn't he?' Max commented with dry irony.

Her eyes stabbed the same irony back at him. 'Like Madeleine gets to you.'

His mouth twisted into a grimace and he turned his gaze away, staring down at the water again. Helen did not find the silence un-comfortable. It was oddly companionable. She watched the little waves lap the hull of the ferry, her mind deliberately emptied of thought.

'Yes, she still does.'

Helen glanced at Max in surprise. The words had been dragged out reluctantly and he was shaking his head as if wanting to disown the admission. He looked at her, his eyes filled with self-mockery.

'And that's after ten years, not four.'

Curiosity prompted her to ask, 'What went wrong?'

He gave a short, derisive laugh. 'What didn't?

We screwed each other up so much that there was no possible point of return. She's the only woman I've ever loved, but she's always been a black-hearted bitch.'

'Always, Max?' Helen questioned softly.

He took one last puff on his cigar and tossed it away, watching it arc and sizzle into the water. 'Maybe not so much then,' he muttered. 'An eye for an eye, a tooth for a tooth, and a bed for a bed . . . Madeleine's code of justice.'

Helen leapt to the obvious conclusion. 'You were unfaithful to her.'

Again came that smile of irony. 'About a thousand times in Madeleine's warped mind, but only once in actuality, and only then because I was accused of it anyway.'

He sighed and brooded down at the water. 'She was so insanely jealous. For no reason. No real reason. I was more of a theatrical agent in those days, building up contacts to break into the big-time. There were always beautiful women around and of course I looked at them. I like beautiful women. But I loved Madeleine. She was an incredible person, so full of a zest for life and everything in it. The only flaw was her jealousy. She'd fly into a rage if she thought I was paying too much attention to another woman. I couldn't seem to be able to reassure her enough.'

He made a short sound of disgust. 'It irritated me, the constant nagging about other women. I was asked to be a judge of a beauty contest and I accepted. Caroline was a contestant and she made a dead set at me. Probably thought it'd help her chances. I wasn't interested in her but do you think Maddie would believe that? Oooh no! We had a full-scale row at the party after Caroline won the title and Maddie stalked out in high dudgeon. I got myself pretty sloshed. Caroline was all too ready to console me and we ended up in bed. Maddie turned up and found us there. She didn't say a word. Just looked and left.'

His hands gestured the hopelessness of the situation. 'I felt sick. I'd really done it. Given her proof of all her suspicions. Anyway, I fronted up at her apartment the next morning, intending to grovel for forgiveness. Maddie was stark naked when she opened the door. She invited me into her bedroom as if nothing had happened. There was another man in her bed and she blithely said that she hoped I didn't mind sharing her with him.'

He shook his head at the memory which still had the power to bring pain to his voice. 'I left. Then I capped the whole damned mess by going off and marrying Caroline. Stupid, stiff-necked pride. I hated Caroline by the end of the honeymoon. Silly empty-headed woman. Every time she opened her mouth my mind screamed for Maddie. It was all so bloody stupid, and marrying Caroline was the unforgivable sin. I should've accepted that Maddie was only paying me back. We should've squared off that morning and let it go. But we've gone on stabbing each other over the years. It's become a habit, a compulsive competition . . . who can get in the most hits. Still a matter of pride, I guess.'

The excursion into the past had brought a mood of tristesse which kept them silent for a while. Helen mused over the remarkable parallels in their separate loves; the long build-up of jealousy and possessiveness climaxing in acts of rebellion, both centred around a beauty contest, one cataclysmic night which severed the relationship, and then the long hangover of hurt, never really healing.

'Do you still love her, Max?' Helen asked sympathetically.

He straightened and gave a little shrug. 'I don't think you'd call it love any more. Too much water under the bridge.' He reached over and took one of her hands, fondling it gently as he spoke. 'Maybe I'm feeling my age, but I'm sick of one-night stands and meaningless relationships. I want a settled kind of contentment in my life. I like you, Helen. I really do. I feel I can share a lot of good things with you.' He glanced sharply at her. 'Is Joe going to get in the way?'

Helen frowned, suddenly realising that Max was not quite the person she had thought him. He had added several dimensions tonight and this last speech cast a new light on her most troublesome doubts. 'What are you saying, Max? That you're through chasing other women?'

'If you marry me. I want our marriage to work, Helen. I want you to be happy with me, to feel secure in our relationship. I'll go to any reasonable length to ensure that. And I think I am a reasonable man,' he added on a softly ironical lilt.

He was sincere. Quite clearly sincere. She did not have to fear the effect of infidelities if she married him. They could have a compatible life together and their understanding of each other was far better now than when she had accepted his proposal earlier tonight. And Joe? Joe was a four-year-old fantasy which had exploded on her tonight with the same destructive force which had ended their relationship. But she was not going to let him destroy what she had now. She turned to Max.

'Will you kiss me . . . please?'

He gently cupped her face with his hands and his eyes were soft with understanding. 'This is me, Helen. Not Joe.'

His mouth tasted faintly of cigars but his kiss was tenderly persuasive. It was a kiss of caring, of comfort and sympathy, a promise that all would be well, given time.

'Thank-you,' she whispered.

He smiled and brushed her cheek with a fingertip caress. 'My pleasure.'

'I will marry you, Max,' she said decisively.

His smile broadened. 'I must practise that kiss.'

She gave a self-conscious little laugh. 'It wasn't just the kiss. I do like you, Max. Very much. There is one thing though . . .'

'Mmmh?'

'I wish . . . I mean . . .' She looked anxiously at him. '. . . Would you stop using me to get at Madeleine? I don't want to be part of that.'

He heaved a sigh and spread his hands in an apologetic gesture. 'Was it so obvious to you?'

She nodded. 'Your attention was always focussed on her reaction.'

'I'm sorry, Helen. I hope you didn't feel . . . well . . . downgraded. No more Madeleine. Only you. I promise.'

'I would be grateful,' she muttered, hoping that Madeleine would cease hostilities once she realised that Max had retired from the battle. Helen's mind shied clear of Joe and she did not want him thrust at her by Madeleine Kane. He had to be blocked out. Somehow.

'Well, gratitude is not to be sneezed at,' Max declared blithely and tucked her arm into his, his old debonair manner suddenly restored. 'Shall we rejoin the party? I ordered a '67 D'Yquem. Marvellous wine. It should certainly sweeten the rest of the evening for us.'

'If you say so,' she smiled, not at all confident that anything could sweeten it, but determined to put as good a face on it as she could manage. 'Do I look a mess?'

'Never!' He grinned. 'Besides, it will make Keith envious. Just for the record, how many "nos" did he get from you?'

'Four,' she stated flatly, wishing Max had not asked that question. It recalled what she was trying to forget.

Max's eyebrows shot up in surprise. 'He really did fancy you. The man has better taste than I thought.'

'I don't like him, Max.'

'Ah, but you don't really know him.' The dark eyes were suddenly shadowed with a world-weary knowledge. 'Remind me to tell you about his ex-wife sometime. Most of my friends are the walking wounded who have had the will to survive. You have that same quality, Helen. We'll survive, you and I, because it's what we both want and we'll make it so.'

'Yes, we'll make it so,' she agreed with quiet determination, cementing the bond between them, yet unable to shake off the sadness which his words had provoked.

Max steered her back into the dining-room and Helen did not care if the eyes which swung towards them found something amiss in her appearance. The newly-forged bond between herself and Max formed a protective wall around her. She was a person to him, not a piece of art, and she now felt assured that it was really the person that mattered. The vital spark of love might be missing from their relationship but perhaps mutual respect was a better basis for marriage. At the very least they would appease each other's loneliness.

She glanced apprehensively towards the table, hoping that Joe would not make the evening more difficult than it had already become. Madeleine was not beside him and Helen glanced quickly around the dining-room without spotting her anywhere. Like the rest of the party, Joe was perusing the menu again, apparently with nothing on his mind except choosing a sweet dish.

'Well, I'm going to have the raspberry soufflé,' Penny Chissolm declared brightly, catching sight of Max and Helen at the same instant. 'Aha! The love-birds return! We shan't have to send out life-boats after all, Bart.'

Her husband reacted with an arch look of surprise. 'Thought you two had fallen overboard.'

'You haven't a romantic bone in your body, Bart,' Cheryl Danvers chided him, her big brown eyes dewy with sentimentality as they cast their approval on Max and Helen before sliding to the adored Jimmy.

'Romance? Huh!' Keith Farrell chortled at the very thought.

'There is something about moonlight on water which stirs the senses,' Max stated blandly as he drew out Helen's chair for her.

'Not to mention something more soft and rounded,' Keith drawled. 'I don't think I've ever seen you look quite so . . . inviting, Helen.'

'One should never presume an invitation, Keith. And I don't care for gate-crashing. Do you?'

He laughed at her provocative retort but Helen wasn't laughing. That was precisely what Joe had attempted . . . gate-crashing four whole years. A well of resentment rose at the memory of his presumption and she flicked a hostile glance at him. Four years had built strong defences but she was not armed against the despair which flowed out of the dark eyes, engulfing her in its pain. It shook her. It shook her so much that a temporary escape was mandatory. Instead of sitting down she picked up her evening-bag and flashed a bright smile to cover her inner agitation.

'If you'll excuse me, Max, I think I'll go and put myself in order before Keith thinks up any more little teasers.'

Max laughed and winked at Keith. 'Here's one woman who's got your measure, Keith. Give up, my friend.' He scooped a menu from the table and offered it to Helen. 'Want to choose a sweet before you go?'

'You choose for me, Max,' she said quickly and made her retreat with all the dignity she could muster.

The vanity section of the Powder Room was unoccupied. One of the toilet cubicles was closed, indicating someone else's presence but one woman was not a nattering group. Helen was relieved to find herself virtually alone. She desperately needed some time to herself.

The wall above the wash-basins was all mirror, harshly lit by fluorescent lights. Helen's reflection jumped back at her; face shiny, lips bare of colour, hair mussed from its usual smoothness, a slight smudge of mascara under her lower lashes . . . but it was the eyes which unnerved her, eyes haunted by Joe's despair.

Was she wrong? Did Joe really love her? Helen closed the tortured eyes and rubbed agitatedly at her temples. No, it could not be. He would have come back. But Mrs Torelli had not told him about her visit. He had not known that she still wanted him. Oh God! What was the answer?

She dragged her eyes open and despite her slight dishevelment, beauty looked back at her from the mirror. And there was the answer. It would always come between them. She knew it and Joe knew it. That was at the root of his despair . . . the root of all the misunderstandings which had led her into that fateful contest and the years that had followed . . . insurmountable barriers to ever reclaiming the unquestioned love which had once been theirs.

What she had to do now was build defences which would see her through the remainder of the evening. Somehow she had to bear Joe's continued presence and keep her emotions in check. Max would help her. It was very comforting to know that she could now rely on Max. He would give her loyalty in a far more personal sense than she had ever anticipated from him.

Quite mechanically she set to work, restoring the image of perfection which was her first line of defence. She had just removed the smudge of mascara when the door of the toilet cubicle opened. The woman had a hand to her forehead obscuring her features, but there was no mistaking the shock of red hair. Madeleine leaned against the wall just outside the cubicle and dragged the hand down her face. The heavy eyelids seemed to lift with reluctance and only then did she see Helen.

'Are you all right, Madeleine?'

Instantly the dulled eyes flared into glittering life. 'Yes.' The word was hissed, squeezed out between clenched teeth. The vivid red mouth twisted into an ugly line. 'Go ahead. Make yourself more beautiful. You've got Max and Joe. Keith if you crooked a finger at him. And I doubt Jimmy or Bart would say no. Why don't you take on the whole damned table?'

Helen sucked in a deep breath and let it out slowly. There was no way to counter the venom in Madeleine's speech. All she could do was retain her own dignity. 'I'm sorry,' she muttered and turned back to the mirror.

'Don't you dare offer me sympathy, you mealy-mouthed chit. You make me sick! You've got it so damned easy, haven't you? You don't even have to work at it. A visual piece of art . . . skin-deep!'

It took all of Helen's will-power not to react violently to those words . . . a piece of art . . . Joe's words. The blistering contempt was par for the course from Madeleine, but the thought that Joe had talked about her in those terms to this bitch of a woman stirred a revulsion that could barely be contained. But she would not give Madeleine the satisfaction of knowing she had drawn blood. With every ounce of control she could command, Helen opened her evening-bag, took out a comb and began tidying her hair, studiously ignoring the other woman.

'Nothing to say!' Madeleine mocked viciously. 'But then you don't need to be able to talk, do you? Your body says it all for you.'

Helen's hand trembled but it kept on combing until every last strand of hair was smoothly in position. Madeleine had not spoken again. Neither had she moved from her position against the wall. Helen could not help flashing a resentful glance at the other woman's reflection as she put the comb away and fumbled for her lipstick.

The green eyes had a glazed look. They drifted slowly down the thin body. A hand lifted and rubbed at the protrusion of hip-bone which interrupted the line of the straight black dress. The red fingernails spread out, examining the underfleshed rib-cage before gliding over small breasts to the angular knob of shoulder. The bleak expression of despair on the white face was terrible to see. Helen looked away, embarrassed by the revelation of a Madeleine stripped of her bristling armour. But the image held a dreadful fascination. Against her will Helen's eyes were drawn back, compelled to look again.

One long finger rubbed at the wrinkles around the green eyes, stretching the skin to eradicate the age-lines. The fluorescent lights were merciless. The mirror was ruthless in reflecting the truth. The finger ran slowly down the too-strong nose and traced around the thin line of lips. The green eyes dulled to a murky grey.

Helen tore her gaze away, ashamed of watching what should not be watched. The pain in that wretched physical assessment made her feel guilty for having been favoured with beauty. It was so unfair that she should unwittingly make another woman feel inferior or inadequate in comparison. But nothing was fair in this world. Beauty had its disadvantages too. The trouble was, no-one ever believed that.

Helen put her lipstick away and clicked her evening-bag shut. The sound snapped Madeleine out of her introspection.

'All polished up for the next round,' she jeered.

Helen gazed steadily back at the white face in the mirror. 'I'm not fighting you, Madeleine.'

Madeleine's face suddenly contorted with hatred. Her arm lifted and a black missile whipped past Helen's head and smashed into the mirror, shattering it so that long, jagged shards of glass broke off and fell on to the washstand, showering the small black handbag which had caused the damage.

'I hate your Goddamned beautiful face! And I hate your ripe young body! Bits of flesh . . . that's all they are. Bits of flesh!'

Madeleine bit the words out with intense passion and the most frightening part of their delivery was the low, vibrant tone. Not a scream. Not a violent hurling of voice to match the thrown handbag. A slow, paced statement of fact.

Shock held Helen rigid as Madeleine advanced on her. The black-clad body swayed like a snake and the green eyes were hypnotic in their feverish glitter.

'What if that face was carved up? Do you think you could hold a man then? A man like Max?' Her hand darted out and snatched up a long shard of glass. A weird little laugh gurgled out of her throat as she fingered the edge for sharpness. 'Maybe I should perform a piece of negative plastic surgery on the golden girl. Reveal the gobby clay underneath. Max wouldn't like that. He likes gold, you see. Can't resist pretty, gleaming things. Fool's gold! Junk!'

'You're mad,' Helen whispered. Her throat was very, very dry. Common sense shrieked that she should turn and leave instantly but her shocked brain was sluggish in sending its message to her legs.

'Mad, am I? Would you like to put that to the test, my beauty?'

The jagged piece of mirror was lifting. Helen stared at it, mesmerised by the reflection of red fingernails which wild imagination transformed into globulets of blood. Helen could not believe, simply could not bring herself to believe this was happening. It was almost as if she was outside this scene looking on. Then the edge of glass was against her cheek, cold reality sending a chill right through her. The vicious mockery in the green eyes added its more lethal chill. Helen's heart felt like a frozen lump, all animation suspended.

'One long scar to mar that perfection and Max would turn away. Only the best for Max. You know that. If you know him at all.'

The soft, throaty sneer held a compelling persuasion and for one self-destructive moment, Helen welcomed the imminent scarring, welcomed the end of a beauty which had seemed a curse to her in so many ways. Let it be so, she thought fatalistically, but on the heels of that thought rose the powerful instinct for self-preservation. She jerked her head back and grabbed Madeleine's wrist, thrusting it away. Her tongue found voice and cut through the dangerous spell Madeleine had woven.

'You crazy fool! Do you think Max would turn to you if you hurt me? Haven't you learnt anything over the years? You drive him further away with each wound you inflict.'

'You know nothing! Nothing about Max and me!' Madeleine hissed.

'Oh, yes I do, Madeleine. I know all about you. Max and I have no secrets from each other,' Helen threw back in reckless counter-attack, driven beyond discretion by the fright Madeleine had given her. 'You're sick! You're just as sick as Joe, unable to accept what's under your nose because your mind's all twisted up with your own insecurities. You choked off what you could have had with Max just as blindly as Joe choked off what he could have had with me. So give up! It's over! Max wants me and I want him and nothing you can do or say is going to change our minds.'

The fire in Madeleine's eyes had dimmed under the force of Helen's tirade but it suddenly blazed anew. 'A pretty face can't fulfil Max's needs.'

'I'm not just a pretty face!' Helen retorted fiercely.

The red mouth snarled in contempt. 'Oh, yes you are! You're like all the rest. A whole parade of pretty faces. And I don't need this to cut you out of Max's life.' She wrenched her arm out of Helen's hold and tossed the piece of mirror on to the vanity.

It was too much. The last straw. Madeleine's contempt, Joe's obsession, Keith, the millions of eyes which had seen the surface and looked no further . . . Helen snapped. Like a claw her hand reached out and grabbed Madeleine's shoulder, pulling the woman around to face her.

'I am not just a pretty face,' she grated out through the clenched teeth of fury, then exploded into wild rage. 'Why the hell should I accept your judgment and punishment? What am I guilty of? Having a face and figure that you want? You think I've got it all. A flick of the finger and the world is at my feet. What world, Madeleine? Men who see me only as a sex object, and women who hate my guts because of it. Do you envy that?'

Her other hand took hold and she shook Madeleine just as her voice shook with scorn. 'Do you really envy that? To be seen as a body and nothing else? To have this barrier of flesh between you and everyone else? God! You don't know what it's like! And you don't care. Nobody cares because I'm so damned beautiful, aren't I? I've got it all!'

Helen shook her again, even more wildly as the pent-up frustration of years boiled over. 'All of what? What, Madeleine? What have I got all of? Love? Respect? Understanding? Real friendships? Is that what flows to me from the whole table?'

She released Madeleine with a contemptuous little push. 'You disgust me with your mean little mind. I feel the same pain you do, and I'm through turning the other cheek to such as you. So watch your tongue, Madeleine. You give me my just due as a fellow human being or you can forget about socialising with Max.'

The fight which had been knocked out of Madeleine by Helen's blitzing tirade, snapped back into gear. She assumed a bearing of haughty disdain. 'You silly, vain cow. If you think you can dictate to Max, you're even more of a doll full of sawdust than I took you for. You might hold him for a while but sooner or later you'll pall, and then he'll be looking for the stimulation of my company, just as he always has.'

'Stimulation!' Helen snarled, infuriated even further by Madeleine's insults. 'Is that what you call your nastiness? Well, let me tell you Max is sick of it. He's marrying me because he enjoys my company. We understand each other, Madeleine. We're happy together. We find each other stimulating in a pleasant way. And it's me he wants to share his life with. Not a vindictive,

jealous bitch who can't accept him for the man he
is.'

Madeleine had turned aside to pick up the
black evening-bag. There was a moment of
stillness and then she slowly wheeled around, her
chin lifted high, eyebrows arched in mockery.
'He married Caroline too. It means less than
nothing. You see, my dear Helen, Max is mine.
He's always been mine on a level you'll never
understand, and he always will be mine because
we're part of each other and I'll never let him go.'

She leaned past Helen and opened the door.
Helen's hand shot out and grabbed her wrist,
halting any further movement. She was not
taking any more of Madeleine's condescension.

'Oh, I understand, Madeleine,' she dripped out
acidly. 'You're part of Max all right. Just as Joe's
a part of me. But you're parts we want to forget.
And we will, Madeleine, because we'll have each
other. Go on and do your worst, but you won't
take Max from me. I want him. I need him. And
I'm going to keep him.'

Green eyes clashed with blue, contemptuous
fire meeting icy determination, and the fire
flickered uncertainly for a moment before blazing
anew.

'You may try, my dear, but I don't have to
paint and groom myself to keep him.' And on
that mocking note she snatched her hand out of
Helen's grasp and made a swift exit.

The door closed. Helen sagged against the
wall, trembling now from nervous reaction to the

emotional forces which had raged through her. It took a tremendous effort of will to pull herself under control.

All right. All right, she repeated insistently. Nothing's changed. It's just all out in the open now. All the undercurrents which had been simmering beneath the surface ever since Max's announcement. Joe wanted her. Madeleine wanted Max. But neither of them had done anything positive about making their desires known until tonight. Like dogs in the manger they had climbed out of the woodwork to ruin what should have been a happy night for Helen and Max. And even now, neither of them could offer anything but a miserable life. Max and she had made their decision. Tonight was the turning point. No more looking back to could-have-beens.

Her gaze drifted over the mess of glass on the wash-stand. Broken glass ... broken loves ... broken lives. Time to pick up the pieces and move on. With a renewed sense of determination Helen pulled some paper towels from the dispenser and swept the dangerous litter into the far corner of the wash-stand.

Then she examined her reflection in the undamaged section of the mirror. Her face was pale but composed. So her beauty had attracted Max. There was no denying that. But it had not drawn his proposal. Madeleine was mistaken in her judgment. Badly mistaken. And Helen was going to do her damnedest to prove that to her from now on. That black-hearted bitch would be shown that the doll was not full of sawdust.

Ever since Joe had cast her out Helen had been carrying a load of guilt which she had subconsciously accepted. But not any more. She had as much right to happiness as anyone else. And neither Joe nor Madeleine was going to take that from her.

With angry pride she challenged her own eyes in the mirror. So you're beautiful! You don't have to make a cage for yourself with the rest of the world on the other side. Nor do you have to tamely accept prods from people like Madeleine. It flashed through her mind that she had already broken out of the mould of the past few years . . . making stands against Keith and Joe and now Madeleine. The thought gave her satisfaction. She could handle it. She could handle anything.

And on that note of self-determination Helen opened the door of the Powder Room and strode out to meet the whole world head on.

CHAPTER SIX

HELEN met the eyes which turned up to her with a smile. Max had said that looking at her gave him pleasure, so why shouldn't be she pleased that she gave the same visual pleasure to others. She walked with pride and confidence past the tables and her smile grew in brightness as Jimmy Danvers rose to hold her chair.

His eyes sparkled over her with a gleam of sexual appraisal and she accepted that too. It wasn't really personal. He loved Cheryl. It was simply a compliment to her appearance, a man telling a woman that she looked desirable, that she had, in fact, achieved what she had meant to achieve with this dress.

'Thanks, Jimmy,' she said warmly.

Cheryl leaned forward, heaving an envious sigh. 'I wish I could wear a dress like that. You look absolutely super in it, Helen.'

Helen stifled the instinctive reaction to play herself down and forced a laugh to her lips. 'Only Max could have persuaded me into it.' She flashed him a flirtatious look. 'He likes me in daring clothes, just as I'm sure Jimmy likes you in feminine clothes.'

Cheryl preened, fingering a frill as she batted her eyelashes at Jimmy. 'Yes, he does, don't you, darling?'

'I sure do, honey-bun,' he grinned and dropped a kiss on her curls as he sat down again.

'I wonder that you could call that a dress at all,' Madeleine said waspishly. 'It covers so little of you.'

'Ah, but promises much,' Max said with meaningful relish.

Helen flicked a derisive look at Joe and Madeleine as she turned to grin at Max. Let them think what they liked, she told herself firmly. The die had been cast and they were not going to influence her behaviour any more. Max's attitude towards her made life a lot less complicated. He had no hang-ups which made her feel bad.

The drink-waiter was hovering at his elbow. The pleasure on Max's face shifted from Helen to the wine as the '67 D'Yquem was poured. He waited until Helen's glass had been filled then lifted his to sniff the bouquet.

'Mmmh . . . unbelievable. Try it.'

Helen followed his example. 'It's very rich, isn't it? Like heavily scented flowers,' she murmured appreciatively.

Max smiled his approval. 'Exactly. And look at that magnificent colour . . .' He lifted his glass to the light. 'Pink-gold.'

'Pink?' Keith scoffed critically. 'Orange-gold, old boy. Your eyes deceive you.'

'Who cares?' Jill Amory pouted, obviously fed up with wine-talk and the indulgences of connoisseurs.

Keith turned on her, the pale blue eyes glacial. 'We are discussing a '67 D'Yquem.'

'Endlessly,' Jill muttered, either unaware of the depth of Keith's displeasure or too annoyed to retreat.

The look of distaste on Keith's face suggested that Jill Amory had just eliminated herself from his favour. 'I do not mind your ignorance, my dear, but I would be obliged if you did not display it quite so publicly,' he said with a cutting edge of contempt.

Helen shrank back in sympathy with the poor girl. Jill had been unwise but the crime did not fit the punishment of being publicly humiliated. Helen's dislike of Keith Farrell moved up a notch. She glanced an appeal at Max to gloss over the nasty moment but his eyebrow was cocked at Keith in a 'well, what can you expect?' expression. It was Joe who came to the rescue.

'I'm almost afraid to show my ignorance,' he said drily. 'But I find the taste of this wine so rich as to be almost cloying.'

The focus of attention switched to him. Keith and Max were only too pleased to extend Joe's knowledge with a dissertation on the subtleties of fruit and age. Helen watched Joe respond in the same easy manner he had employed at the table all night. The despair which had disturbed her so much was no longer in evidence. Which was a relief. She did not want to be disturbed by Joe any more.

Her gaze drifted to Madeleine who was

downing the contents of her glass with a notable absence of reverence for what she was drinking. It drew a frown of censure from Max.

'You are inordinately thirsty, Madeleine,' he chided.

'This wine suits me. After all, I'm a fruity old hag.'

The tone and content of the remark caused another little silence around the table. To speak slightingly of herself was particularly un-characteristic and the words had been rolled out with harsh emphasis, in marked contrast to the usual fine stiletto of her tongue. But Madeleine had spoken for just such an effect. The mocking green eyes stabbed that point home to Helen. Fruity old hag she might be, but she didn't need a daring dress to draw Max's eye. Her voice could do that.

Again it was Joe who slid into the slight impasse. 'I doubt that your worst enemy would call you an old hag, Madeleine,' he said in an amused tone. 'If we're to compare you to this wine, I'd say the likeness lies in the richness of complexity.'

Madeleine's smile was saccharin-sweet. 'How kind you are, Joe! But kindness can be very cloying. A good word, cloying. That's what we are, Joe. Did you know that? So cloying that we choke people.'

The venomous look she turned on Helen gave full warning of a no-holds-barred war and she was going to use their argument in the Powder

Room for ammunition. Well, so be it, Helen thought belligerently. The bitch can have her own fire straight back. With interest.

'One could hardly accuse you of choking people with sweetness, Madeleine,' Helen commented pointedly.

'Nor kindness,' Joe added, and there was a note of intense regret in the words.

The soft reprimand surprised and silenced Madeleine. She shot Joe a glare which he met head-on.

'No more,' he murmured, then turned to Keith with a question about the wine industry in Australia.

Madeleine's lips thinned in frustration and she snatched up her glass and drank as if she needed more fortification since her ally had deserted her.

Helen did not imagine for one moment that Madeleine would be moved from her malicious purpose but she was completely stunned by Joe's swing to her defence. She stared at him, wondering what he was really feeling under the facade of interest he was showing to Keith. There had been regret in his voice. Regret for the hurt he had given her? Had he finally understood how wrong he'd been?

Helen wrenched her eyes away and fixed them on her own glass. 'Or kindness.' The words echoed around her mind. Joe was essentially kind. It was one of the things Helen had loved about him; the good-humoured way he would settle spats among his younger brothers and sisters so that no one felt put out or badly done by, his thoughtfulness towards others' feelings, soothing a hurt ego or cheering up a gloom. Even tonight he had played Madeleine's game so that she could save face. And just now smoothing over Jill's gaffe by mocking his own ignorance, thereby minimising the spotlight on hers.

Helen could not remember Joe's hurting anyone but herself, the woman he supposedly loved, and that had been a monstrous, damning hurt. 'I didn't like the person I was turning into any more than you did.' That's what he'd said and Helen realised that he had spoken the truth. A kind person wouldn't like to see himself doing what he had done to her. He had suffered from his actions, probably as much as she. Compassion for his self-torment softened her heart. If only he had told her then . . .

No, it wouldn't have changed anything, reason insisted. His obsession with her beauty would have blocked his ears, just as it had clogged the natural impulses of his heart. It would always have come between them. It still did. Joe's obsession. Madeleine's jealousy. Seeds of destruction to any promise of happiness.

'Aha!' Jimmy Danvers drawled loudly. 'It looks like our Creme Caramels are on the way, Cheryl.'

The announcement snapped Helen out of her introspection. She had to stop thinking about Joe and the past. She was going to marry Max.

The waiter placed a strawberry tartlet in front

of Helen. It looked delectable. An apricot glaze gave the strawberries a luscious sheen and the surrounding pastry was fluted to crisp perfection.

'Did I make the right choice?' Max asked.

She smiled at him. 'Lovely choice. In fact it looks so perfect it's almost a pity to cut into it.'

He chuckled and shook his head at her. 'However much pride the chef may have taken in its perfection, I doubt that he'd appreciate having it returned in one piece.'

'I always thought pastry gave people pimples,' Madeleine remarked sweetly. 'How do you manage such a perfect complexion, Helen?'

So! Madeleine was on the attack again! Helen's hackles rose and her reply was equally sweet. 'I put a mixture of egg-white and mud on my face every night.'

'You don't!' came Cheryl Danvers' shocked voice. 'Oh, you couldn't, Helen!'

'She's pulling your leg, Cheryl,' Penny Chissolm explained wearily.

'Oh, I didn't think that Max would want to go to bed with . . . oh!' Cheryl retired in a fluster of embarrassment while everyone laughed at the image conjured up.

Everyone but Madeleine. 'No. I doubt that mud and egg-white would appeal to a sybarite like Max,' she said waspishly. 'But then, Helen has so much else that appeals.'

'A great deal else,' Max agreed with a warmth which dispelled the nastiness of Madeleine's implication. 'She has been, for some time now, a

woman I value in every possible sense. And
Cheryl, let me tell you, if Helen wished to mask
her face in any manner whatsoever, it would not
lessen her value to me one tiny bit.'

A rush of gratitude swamped Helen's heart.
Max's support was all she could have wished and
Madeleine could have received very little satisfaction from his reply to her taunt. It left her little
ground for the contention that Helen's attraction
was purely physical.

But Madeleine had either found Max's words
too unpalatable to swallow or her spite had grown
too bilious to contain. 'How gallant you are,
Max!' she sniped. 'One could almost believe you.'

The green eyes glittered with anticipation as
Max turned to her and Helen suddenly knew that
Madeleine had deliberately thrown down the
gauntlet. The claws were out and blood was
going to flow. Helen's nerves screeched danger.
Danger of what she did not know but Madeleine
was projecting the wild, reckless air of a wounded
animal who was intent on fighting to the death.
Acting on sheer instinct, Helen reached out a
hand to stop Max from taking up the challenge.
She squeezed his arm hard.

'Please ignore it, Max,' she whispered urgently.
'She doesn't bother me.'

But he was too incensed. 'Hell no!' he grated,
and his face settled into the same look of cold
distaste that Keith Farrell had turned on to Jill
Amory. He addressed Madeleine in a tone which
dripped acid.

'I would not expect you to believe me, Madeleine. You never did have any faith in anything but yourself. But your belief or disbelief does not alter the truth. I doubt that you have the generosity of spirit to make a genuine apology so I shall not demand it. But don't slight my regard for Helen again if you wish to retain my friendship, such as it is.'

The snub was icily deliberate as he turned his attention to the rest of the party. 'I would have thought that the announcement of my forth-coming marriage was indicative enough that Helen is a very special lady to me. I did not anticipate that surprise would breed scepticism. However, to prevent any such mistake from arising again, I inform you all here and now, that Helen has my deepest esteem and affection.'

'And rightly so,' murmured Jimmy Danvers.

'Well said, old boy,' Keith said with a rueful little smile.

'A pity you couldn't have tape-recorded that, Helen,' Penny Chissolm said with a touch of whimsy. 'When you've been married as long as I have, you rarely get to hear such a lovely declaration.'

'Ooooh, what a rotten little ingrate you are!' Bart protested. 'I've done much better than that in my time. Poetry and hearts and flowers . . . even serenades.'

They bantered on with their well-oiled routine, covering Madeleine's rout. Max had placed himself unequivocally at Helen's side and in doing it so very publicly, he had pulled Madeleine's fangs, once and for all. Nothing could have been more decisive in killing any hope which Madeleine might have nursed that Max would eventually turn to her.

The woman's face was a white blank. All her vitality had drained away. There was a stillness about her which was corpse-like. A little shiver ran down Helen's spine but she quelled the instinctive rise of pity. Madeleine herself had been pitiless. Yet there was something dreadful in the totality of her defeat.

Helen could not feel comfortable about it. She wished . . . she wished Max had not reacted with quite so much venom. She remembered all too well what it was like to have one's spirit completely crushed and she did not wish that on anyone. Not even Madeleine who would probably have had no compunction in doing it to Helen.

'When are you getting married, Max?'

It was Joe's voice, calm, deliberate, cutting through the nonsense at the other end of the table. The question sparked off a flurry of remarks.

'Yes, when's the date? We'll have to get our glad rags out,' from Penny Chissolm.

'And where's it to be? Always wanted to put on a wedding in our garden,' Jimmy Danvers declared smugly.

'Well, I claim the right to be best man,' Keith Farrell boomed out. 'By God, Max! We'll open some bottles that day.'

'That we will, Keith,' Max agreed, his good humour quickly restored. 'It'll be after the Joel Thomas tour. Helen and I are pretty busy until then. When we set a date we'll let you all know. And Jimmy, that garden idea sounds good. What do you think, Helen?'

She shrugged off her disquiet and forced a smile. 'Yes. It sounds lovely,' she agreed, yet not really caring what they did. Which pricked at her sense of rightness. This was her wedding they were discussing. Her marriage. To Max. She should be excited. Looking forward to it. Damn Joe and Madeleine for spoiling it for her!

'It'll be a few weeks then.'

It was Joe asking the question again. She glanced sharply at him. Why did he want to know? His expression was impenetrable and Helen realised with a jolt that she no longer knew this man intimately and could not predict what his questions portended.

'Yes. A few weeks,' Max affirmed casually, but his eyes also were probing for Joe's intentions. 'You can be sure we won't waste any time in getting together. As Madeleine pointed out earlier. I'm not getting any younger.' It was a subtle warning.

Joe's mouth took on a wry twist. 'The end of anything seems more real when there's a definite date,' he mused softly, the words only audible to Madeleine, Max and Helen. 'It's difficult to let go a dream one has lived with for a long time. The day you and ... Helen marry will be a release for me. The past must then be relegated to the past for there can be no hope of its ever forming part of the future.'

Colour suddenly burnt into Madeleine's cheeks, giving them a feverish look. 'You're a fool, Joe,' she hissed contemptuously.

He shook his head at her and his eyes were sad. 'No, Madeleine. Fools keep dreaming. I have been a fool. If I'd been less of a one I would've made the woman I love happy.'

Helen felt her heart being squeezed, yet this was what she wanted, wasn't it? For Joe to give up and go away? To release her from the emotional chaos he stirred? It was what she had asked of him . . . if he loved her. If he loved her. Her heart contracted again, even more tightly. My God! Was she making a terrible mistake in turning her back on Joe?

She felt Max's eyes on her, a sharp probe she was in too much turmoil to meet. She kept her gaze fixed on the glass in her hand. He reached out and stroked her wrist and she sensed it was a gesture of unease, but for the life of her she could not send him a confident look of reassurance.

'I'd like to think that you'll make . . . Helen happy, Max,' Joe said quietly, again using her full name as if distancing himself from the Nell he had loved. 'I hope you appreciate the woman she is.'

'I do,' Max answered shortly, almost tersely.

'Oh, for God's sake! This is a party, isn't it?' Madeleine demanded irritably. 'Fill my glass again, Max.' She raised her voice, injecting it with a brittle gaiety. 'Jimmy, tell us your new jokes. Let's have a laugh.'

Jimmy was only too happy to oblige and once he had set the ball rolling, Bart and Penny Chissolm kept it going. Helen tried to block out the doubts which were seething through her mind but it was impossible. She laughed when the rest of the party laughed but she did not hear one joke. All she heard were the fevered questions which were torturing her heart.

Did Joe love her? Did he really love her? Was he giving up because she had demanded it of him, or had he realised that the emotions stirred by old memories were simply . . . old memories? A time to stop dreaming, he had said.

Her eyes were drawn to him in a compulsive need to know the answer. As if called by her concentrated gaze, Joe looked straight at her and there was no time to adopt masks. Their inner anguish was laid bare to each other, forming a powerful channel of communication through which flowed more than the memories of pain and desolation . . .

A madcap day at Taronga Park zoo . . . a whole afternoon riding the Manly Ferry back and forth across the harbour until an attendant insisted they leave . . . the free symphony concerts at Town Hall . . . the hours and hours spent sprawled on the campus lawn in the shade of the old Moreton Bay fig-tree . . . the joy and the laughter, all the simple pleasures they shared, the instinctive calling of one to the other, the deep satisfaction of their coming together and knowing that this is my man . . . this is my woman . . . we are one.

Yes, oh, yes it had been so. The whole blissful wonder of their love rolled through her memory. But that was before the rot began; before mutual understanding broke into resentful silences, before actions were given twisted motives, before doubt and fear sowed their destructive seeds and ended it all . . .

Finished, sad blue eyes told him.

Is it? the dark eyes challenged.

Helen wrenched her gaze away, shaken by a spurt of panic. Was it possible? What if Joe had changed? No, no, he hadn't changed, her mind insisted. Not where it mattered for their relationship to ever work. His pride had driven her away, and his pride had kept him away from her, and it was probably his pride that wanted her back now. And if she gave in, it would start again . . . the uncertainties, the accusations, the lack of trust . . . She was a fool to let him get at her like this. She was not going to back out of her commitment to Max for a past love which had been so comprehensively tarnished.

Bart Chissolm suddenly sprang to his feet, arms spread wide to command attention. 'I've got it!' he declared triumphantly. 'Listen to this:

There was a young lady of value,
When asked if she'd wed, said I'll have you,
But let it be clear

I am more than veneer
And Max swore that he took a deep view.'

The limerick won boisterous applause and Bart winked his satisfaction. 'How about it, Maxie?'

Max grinned his appreciation and winked back. 'Right on, Bart. I'll pay that one.'

'Then bring on the Napoleon Brandy.'

'Yes. By all means bring on the brandy,' Madeleine echoed sourly.

Unable to resist holding the floor a little while longer, Bart held out his hands for silence and lifted his glass in a toast. 'To Max and Helen. May they always be true blue to each other.'

The others groaned at the ockerism but they drank the toast, all except Madeleine.

Max squeezed Helen's hand. She threw him a smile and caught the question in his eyes. It sickened her to realise that Max had been fully aware that Joe had plunged her into turmoil again. It was unfair to Max who had stood by her so unwaveringly. He deserved a firm assurance of her commitment. She had to give it. Now. A decision which would put Joe forever in the past where he belonged.

'I've been thinking it's a good idea, moving in with you tomorrow. Will you help me, Max?'

He smiled and there was a wealth of satisfaction in the smile. 'I am completely at your disposal. The sooner the better as far as I'm concerned. You know I want to have you with me.'

Helen did not look at Joe. She had to put him

completely out of her mind if she was to have any peace. Tomorrow she would go to live with Max and build a new future; a good, stable future.

'My glass is empty,' Madeleine complained. 'Fill it up for me, Joe.'

He silently complied with her request. Madeleine took a sip then returned the glass to the table, tipping it back and forth so that the liquid slapped around its sides.

'*Tomorrow . . .*' she slurred over the word in mournful derision. '*Tomorrow and tomorrow and tomorrow, creeps in this petty pace from day to day . . .* isn't that how it goes, Joe?'

'Something like that,' he agreed tiredly.

Madeleine heaved a sigh then continued the quotation.

> '*Life is a tale told by an idiot,*
> *Full of sound and fury,*
> *Signifying nothing . . .*

'Isn't that so, Joe?'

'Perhaps.'

She emptied her glass with reckless speed. 'Pour me another, Joe. I have a feeling that I don't want to look tomorrow in the face. Let's blot it out.'

Balloon glasses had been set around the table when Bart's brandy had been delivered. Joe poured a small measure into Madeleine's glass. She swirled it around, staring morosely at it.

'Should be whisky,' she muttered. 'Isn't it whisky you drink at wakes?'

'This is a party, Madeleine, not a wake,' Max reminded her tersely.

Madeleine's lips twisted into a wry smile. 'You have no Irish in you, Max.'

'If you mean that I refuse to wallow among grievances, you're right. Life is for living.'

The green eyes mocked him with glazed weariness. 'Live then. Be happy with your golden girl. I don't begrudge you happiness. Don't begrudge me oblivion.' She took a large sip of brandy, swirled the liquid around the glass again, then drank some more, swallowing it down as if it was a much-needed drug.

Helen fervently wished the night was over. A fighting Madeleine would have been easier to take than this defeated one. Stripped of her bristling armour she was all too human. The pain was showing. It had been in Joe's voice too when he had answered Madeleine. There was no joy in this victory if it could be called that. No joy at all.

She glanced at Max, sensing that he also was disturbed by Madeleine's change of mood. He was frowning. Then in an abrupt move he signalled a waiter and ordered coffee to be brought immediately. The service was prompt and Max indicated that Madeleine's cup be filled first.

'Don't want coffee,' she mumbled and proceeded to drain her almost empty glass.

'I suggest you move that brandy away, Joe. Madeleine's had more than her fair share,' Max said on a note of concern.

'Madeleine is a free agent. It's her choice.

We're all entitled to make our own choice, Max,'
Joe drawled with a fine edge of mockery.

Helen shot him a sharp look of entreaty. 'Please
don't make it worse, Joe.'

'Worse?' The pain in his eyes stabbed her into
silence. 'Nothing could be worse than this.'

Helen tensed. Joe was out of control. Madeleine
was out of control. Dear God! She shouldn't have
spoken of moving in with Max tomorrow. It had
been too telling, like waving a flag over dead
hopes.

'Damn you for a fool!' Max snapped at Joe.
'You're Madeleine's escort. The least you can do
is look after her.'

Joe's chin tilted to a belligerent angle. 'I'm not
responsible for Madeleine or her actions. Look to
yourself, Max. If you care about her, you do
something about it.'

The challenge brought a glare of anger from Max
but he spoke with tight restraint. 'I am trying to
prevent her from getting more intoxicated than
she already is. If you had any kindness in you at
all, you'd have the decency to co-operate.'

Joe's reply was equally flint-like. 'She has the
right to order her life as she sees fit. Just as you
and Nell do. Leave her be. You've left her anyway.'

The stark statement silenced Max and left a
spine-chilling pall over all four of them as they
each faced that truth . . . paths had been chosen
and others rejected, and all their lives would be
changed from this time on.

To Helen's horror she felt no happiness at the

prospect of the future she had chosen for herself, but a cold, cold despair at which had been lost. And she sensed that all four of them felt the same sinking despair . . . of opportunities wasted, never to be within grasp again . . . of time slipping into an irretrievable compartment, locked away, forever sealed. The silence throbbed with a terrible, gut-wrenching finality and a panicky voice inside Helen wanted to say; Stop! Let's all look again. Maybe it can be different. But she did not speak. It was Madeleine who spoke and she spoke with the voice of finality.

''S right. Nothing left,' she intoned gravely. 'Pass the bottle. Joe. Have to toast Max and Helen. Do the right thing.'

Joe sighed and his reply was flat with resignation. 'No. Max is right, Madeleine. Give it a rest. Have some coffee.'

It was over, that dreadful moment. Helen sucked in a deep breath and let it go slowly, trying to relieve the constriction in her chest. But it would not go away. And the panicky voice was still there inside her. She tried to reason with it. Her decision to marry Max was a sensible one. Joe had accepted it. Even Madeleine had now faced up to its validity. She would be happy with Max. Only she did not feel happy. She did not feel happy with any part of this situation. And every nerve in her body was vibrating with tension.

'Can't make a toast with coffee,' Madeleine mumbled. 'Glass is empty. Need a drink.' She placed her hands on the table and pushed herself to her feet, swaying a little with dizziness. She leaned over to grab a bottle. Her hand knocked the cup of coffee and sent its contents spilling over the white linen tablecloth.

'For Chrissake! Sit down, Madeleine. You're disgusting!' Max hissed at her.

Madeleine's body jerked as though he had struck her.

Helen felt even worse. She knew intuitively that Max's anger was not provoked by an act of clumsiness. He was as deeply disturbed by Madeleine's behaviour as Helen had been by Joe's. But she wished he had not spoken so harshly. Again she had the urge to cry 'Stop! This is all wrong!' But everything seemed out of control now, and the whole party's attention had been drawn to Madeleine.

With a trembling hand she picked up the little coffee-cup and set it on its saucer with elaborate care. Then she straightened her back, drawing herself up to her full tallness. She turned a little, facing Max with a dignity which was pathetically frayed by glittering tears and quivering lips. Her long throat moved convulsively. When at last she spoke, the words were slow and very precise.

'Yes. I am disgusting. I've disgusted myself for ten years. And I've hated every minute of it. But it's over now. I'm glad it's over.' She stretched out a hand and brushed Max's shoulder. 'Be happy, Max. I wish you . . . a good life . . . with all my heart.'

Then she was walking away, head held high,

each step one of stately dignity, like a queen on her last walk to the guillotine.

The fanciful thought frightened Helen. I don't like it. I don't like it at all, the panicky voice said. She dragged her gaze back to Max, hoping for some form of reassurance which would ease her mind.

But Max looked sick. There was a tightness about his jaw which suggested clenched teeth, and his eyes were angry with the fierce anger which wanted to deny he was hurting. Madeleine's halting little speech had hit him harder than any vicious dart she might have fired at him.

It had got to all of them. A prickly silence had fallen over the table. It was broken by Jimmy Danvers.

'I didn't like the sound of that, Max,' he said seriously. 'I think you should go after her.'

'Not me, my friend,' Max flashed back at him with taut vehemence. 'That woman is not skewering me any more. She doesn't wish me anything but hell, and you know it. She only spoke one true word. The game is over.'

Penny Chissolm rose to her feet. 'The game, as you put it, was all Madeleine lived for, Max. Maybe you didn't know that but I can assure you it's true. I'll go and see if she's all right.'

A muscle twitched along Max's tight jaw and his skin grew sallow. They all watched Penny go and the silence became thicker with tension.

'Penny's right, old boy,' Keith said with surprising softness. 'Your marriage announcement was a king-hit. No offence to you, Helen, but Madeleine's been one of us for a long time and you were always her focus, Max. She's been knocked cock-eyed and I think . . .'

'No doubt she'll find plenty of ready help to regain her balance,' Max cut in sarcastically. He threw a malevolent look at Joe. 'She always has in the past.'

'Don't look at me to take your place, Max. My attraction for Madeleine was my resemblance to you. I'm neither friend nor lover, just a familiar set of features she wanted to use.'

Max swallowed convulsively as if he was forcing down bile. 'And you were happy to let her use you,' he jeered.

'We were using each other,' Joe stated flatly. His eyes moved to Helen, frankly displaying a depth of feeling which rocked her.

Her head spun. Her breath caught somewhere in her throat. Her heart stopped.

A low whistle came from Jimmy Danvers.

Max grabbed Helen's hand and smashed a fist down on the table. 'No! Helen is going to marry me and no drunken bitch or Johnny-come-lately is going to get in the way.'

Helen's heart was pumping again. Wildly. Chaotically.

'Cool it, Max,' Jimmy Danvers chopped in quickly. 'We're all pleased for you. Helen's a lovely girl. We're just concerned about Madeleine. Under the circumstances I think it best if Cheryl and I take her home with us. I can't see that you'd be much comfort to her, Joe.'

'Madeleine is more than capable of looking after herself,' Max insisted angrily.

'Not tonight,' Bart Chissolm stated with quiet authority.

'Here comes Penny,' Cheryl said hopefully, anxious for this unpleasant scene to be over.

But it won't be, Helen thought despairingly. Joe had her all confused again, and Max was reacting like a man driven to the end of his tether. And too much had been said for the rest of the party to regain a convivial mood.

And it was not over. Penny Chissolm's face was tight with apprehension and her step held the haste of concern as she hurried towards their table. She pulled up beside Madeleine's empty chair and addressed Max in a slightly breathless voice.

'She's locked the Powder Room door and won't let me in. She won't even answer me.'

'Probably being sick,' Max said with an edge of disgust. 'All that brandy on top of the wine would turn anyone's stomach.'

'No! No, Max,' Penny insisted anxiously. 'There were scrabbling noises and ... and a whimper of pain. I'm afraid that she might have fallen and hurt herself. Do come and force the door open.'

The image of long, jagged shards of glass falling on to the wash-stand flashed into Helen's mind. Maybe some had fallen on the floor. She had not looked there when she had tidied up the mess. 'Penny could be right, Max,' she said quickly. 'Madeleine smashed the mirror earlier tonight. I thought I'd cleaned it up but I might have missed some on the floor.'

'She smashed the mirror?' Max repeated, anger and incredulity driving his voice higher.

'She ... she was upset ... trying to ...' Impossible to explain that scene with everyone listening. Helen's voice pitched to urgency. 'What does it matter? I think you'd better go and see that she's all right.'

Max scraped back his chair, his face more grim than Helen had ever seen it. 'Damn the woman!' was all he said but he was on his feet and going.

Joe stood and followed. The two men strode quickly through the dining-room.

Penny fluttered her hands. Her gaze darted around the table, wanting a reassurance which no-one was prepared to give. Then, too agitated to sit down, she gave a nervous little shrug and took off after the men.

No-one at the table made any attempt to restore the atmosphere to normality. A gloom had settled. They all sat and waited. The silence held the tension of expectancy.

'Bloody hell! Some party this turned out to be,' Bart muttered as each minute added another measure of tension.

Then Penny was running towards them, sweeping past startled diners in a headlong rush. Her chalk-white face and frightened eyes telegraphed panic.

'Keith . . .' she called frantically, even before she reached the table. 'Keith, ask if there's a doctor and tell the Captain to get back to the Quay fast. And radio ahead for an ambulance. She's . . . oh, God! She's cut her wrists. There's . . . there's blood everywhere,' she gasped, then burst into tears. Her last message was sobbed out. 'Everyone is to stay here but Helen . . . Helen they want you to help. I can't . . . I can't . . .'

'Shut up, Penny!' Keith ordered harshly. 'Bart, take care of her. It's an accident and don't anyone say any different. The mirror broke and Madeleine got cut. That's the story. I'll do what's necessary. Helen . . . on your way. They must need a woman with them.'

Keith had already moved. Bart was drawing his wife down to her chair, trying to muffle her hysterics. Shock held Helen rigid for a moment longer. And yet in some knowing recess of her mind, she was not shocked. This was the end-game to what had been played out tonight—the danger she had sensed but not identified . . . the panic she had felt as the nails of despair had been hammered home.

Helen forced herself to move. It was fitting that she go there and be with the others . . . with Joe and Max and Madeleine. They were locked into this together and whatever help she could give, had to be given. God help them all . . . because this . . . this could never be forgotten by any of them.

CHAPTER SEVEN

THE door to the Powder Room was slightly ajar. Helen noted the broken catch as she pushed it open. Penny's words had conjured up a more frightful scene than the actual reality, but even so Helen had to quell a wave of nausea.

Madeleine was half-cradled on Max's lap. He was sitting on the tiled floor among broken glass and streaks of blood. One arm was around Madeleine's shoulders, clutching her to him while the other held her left wrist up high, fingers pressing tightly over a wound which still oozed blood. Joe was kneeling beside them, bandaging the other wrist with handkerchiefs which were staining red even as they were tightly tied.

'Do you want more cloth for bandages?' Helen asked, doing her best to sound calm and collected.

Joe glanced around, briefly acknowledging her presence before turning back to his task. 'No. This bleeding will soon stop. It's not too bad. Bandages will be useless on the other wrist. Pressure's better. Will you clean up the glass around us please, Nell?'

Helen set to work. The paper towels which had tidily hidden the mirror fragments were on the floor. In her haste or despair, Madeleine had scattered glass everywhere. Helen carefully lifted it all back on the paper and bundled it into a corner, right out of the way. One of the bowls in the wash-stand was stained with blood. The image of Madeleine crouching over it, watching her lifeblood go down the drain was horribly vivid. In a burst of revulsion Helen flushed the bowl clean, grabbed some more towels, damped them and wiped up every bloodstain she could see.

'Okay, Max. I'll take that wrist now,' Joe said with quiet authority. 'Just hold it steady until I get in a better position.

'Let me go . . .'

The plaintive moan startled Helen. She had thought Madeleine unconscious but the thin body was suddenly restive as Joe released the arm he had tended.

'Be still!' Max snarled down at her.

'Don't . . . don't be angry. Not now.'

The pathetic plea wrung Helen's heart but gained no sympathy from Max.

'Damn you, Maddie!' he retorted fiercely. 'This is the dirtiest trick of all and I'm not going to let you get away with it.'

Tears squeezed out from Madeleine's closed eyelids and trickled into the tumbled profusion of red hair which had torn free of its restraining combs. Max's arm tightened his embrace of her shoulders, pulling her body closer to his, and the desperate anguish on his face belied the harshness of his temper.

'Right, Max. I'm taking over. Ease your fingers away,' Joe instructed.

He had moved around behind them, ready to face anyone who came in the door yet out of the way should a doctor come to help. Helen watched the transfer anxiously. There was only a little gush of blood from the wound before Joe's grip squeezed it shut.

With both arms free Max was able to gentle his hold of Madeleine and Helen could not help but see the loving tenderness in his embrace. He was nursing a woman he loved beyond any barriers which had been set up between them. It was only Madeleine who existed for him in this moment of ultimate stress.

She looked up at Joe, knowing that he was the one in control, knowing also that it had been he who had given the orders to Penny. 'Is there anything else you want me to do?' she asked in a voice she hardly recognised as her own, thin and hollow.

Joe's eyes held an agony of guilt as if he was blaming himself for this tragedy. 'We need someone here to guard the door. Is it . . . is it too much to ask of you?'

'No, of course not. I'll stay,' she replied huskily and swallowed hard in an effort to regain control of her voice.

Her gaze dropped to Madeleine, lying so still now. Am I guilty too, Helen thought uneasily. Did I contribute to this horrible act of self-destruction? But I was only defending myself . . .

myself .... myself ... the word echoed around
her mind, growing louder in its accusation. All
night she had been thinking of herself; how much
she had been hurt, what she wanted from life,
how she wanted to be treated. The brief amount
of pity and compassion she had felt for Joe and
Madeleine had been quickly countered by the
overwhelming chorus of self, self, self.

And now this! My God! What had she done in
her blind selfishness? The taunts she had thrown
back at Madeleine had been cruel stabs at the
hope Madeleine had nursed all these years ... to
have Max on some level ... any level ... and she
had contributed very heavily to the destruction of
that hope.

Her blood is on my hands ... The anguished
thought drew her gaze to the smudges of blood
on Madeleine's arms. Don't die. Please don't die,
she begged. The blood kept magnifying her sense
of guilt, feeding a compulsion to do something,
anything to help.

Her gaze lifted to Joe, pleading for direction.
'Should I clean around that bandage?'

'No. Better to leave her alone now,' he advised,
then shuddered with reaction.

Helen could well appreciate the strain he had
been under since the first few moments of dis-
covery. He sighed and gave her an apologetic look.

'Thanks for coming, Nell. Penny was useless.
Did she give Keith our message?'

'Yes. He sprang into action. I would say
everything's under control. As much as it can be.'

The arm which Joe held upright was almost blue-white. 'Do you know how much blood she's lost?'

'Enough to need a transfusion, that's for sure,' he replied despondently. 'At least we've stopped most of the flow.'

A tap on the door startled them. Helen swung around to meet and turn away any intruder. She put her weight behind the door only to meet firm resistance on the other side.

'It's Keith,' came the peremptory explanation. His bulk squeezed an opening and his head popped around the door. He took in the scene without flickering an eyelid, then grimaced at Max whose attention had been drawn from the woman in his arms. 'Sorry, old boy. No doctor on board, but we're full steam for Circular Quay and we'll have an ambulance waiting there. What's Madeleine's blood type?'

'Maddie, tell me your blood type,' Max demanded anxiously. When she made no reply he took her chin in a punishing grip and steeled his voice to a determined. 'Answer me, Maddie.'

'Let go . . . want to die,' she mumbled.

'No, you don't. You've got to live for me, you stupid, crazy bitch,' he insisted with whip-like severity.

She twisted her head feverishly. 'Don't want me . . . got Helen,' came the weak echo of despair.

Max shot a plea for understanding at Helen. 'No, Maddie, it was always you I wanted. You know that in your heart. You've got to live for me. Tell me your blood type.' Then with growing desperation, 'You're killing me too, Maddie. Tell me!'

'Max . . .' It was a quaver of wretched hope. The eyelids lifted a little as if fighting a terrible lassitude.

'Tell me, damn you!' he shouted hoarsely.

'O . . . type O . . . positive . . . hold me, Max.'

He expelled an emotion-laden breath. 'I'm holding you, Maddie.' He looked up at Keith and there were tears in his eyes. 'Do what you can.'

The big man nodded and departed. Helen pressed the door shut after him and stood with her back to it in case anyone else tried to enter. The harrowing pain in this room was not for curious eyes. It was so dreadfully private that Helen felt herself an intruder.

'Max . . .' Madeleine's throat moved in a convulsive swallow as she reached for strength to speak. The words were forced out in a halting whisper. 'The man . . . in my bed . . . he was a drunk . . . didn't sleep with him . . . just wanted to show you . . . I'm sorry.'

'I know. Not right then but afterwards I knew, Maddie. I was a fool. Don't worry about it now, my love.' He smoothed the tumbled hair away from her temples as he gently crooned to her. 'Remember the good times, Maddie, the fun we had . . . the houseboat on the Hawkesbury River, wasn't that a glorious week?'

'Got burnt,' she whispered but a faint smile quivered on her lips.

'Remember me rubbing cream into your skin. And we made love in between applications. It was so good, Maddie. Just you and I together. You were all I needed, and you were happy with me then. We were wildly happy. Remember catching that big fish . . . and the barbecue we had in the little cove . . . watching the stars come out and wishing for the world to open up for us to take by storm . . . all the dreams we shared, Maddie . . .'

'Dreams . . .'

The word was a dying echo Max's voice was rough with desperation as he continued pleading for his life which could have been.

Helen closed her eyes and tried to block her ears to the intimate outpouring of a love which had been lost . . . no, not lost . . . mislaid in the tortuous maze of emotion which cursed humanity. The memories being so poignantly recalled for Madeleine were so heart-catchingly close to the memories which Joe had forced on Helen, and from the depths of her soul came the cry . . . why did we let it go? Was pride worth the loss?

And the realisation came to her that it had been her pride which had rejected Joe tonight. She had only wanted love on her terms. And with a sickening jolt she saw that she had been at fault in the past too. She also had been blind . . . too self-centred and immature to understand that Joe had needed constant reassurance of her love. She had wanted it all her way . . . her way . . .

Oh, dear God! And it had come to this . . .

wanting to have her way ... and there was Madeleine, so still, so white, so lifeless in Max's arms, and Max silent now, his face drawn with grief for what could have been. He loved Madeleine. He still loved her. And it was a terrible, terrible indictment on human nature that it required the final leveller of death before all could be forgiven and forgotten and the truth laid bare.

And with absolute certainty Helen knew if it was Joe lying there, her arms would be cradling him, begging him to live for her, grieving for the life they could have shared, her heart dying with him because only he had held it and made it beat to a meaningful tune.

A knock close to her ear snapped the reverie of torment.

'Keith again,' came the sharp announcement.

Helen stepped away from the door to give him entrance.

He leaned around it. 'We're almost there. How's Madeleine?'

'She's lost consciousness,' Max stated flatly, a mortal weariness etched deeply on his face.

Keith sucked in a quick breath then spoke with crisp efficiency. 'We'll be taking her off first. No-one will be allowed to move until she's clear. Stretcher will be carried out the back-entrance to the dining-room, then along the side-deck to the gangway. Are you going with her, Max?' he added with a darted look at Helen.

Max lifted pained eyes to her. 'I have to, Helen.'

'I know,' she answered softly. 'Barry will take me home. It's all right, Max.'

He sighed and dropped his gaze to the still figure in his arms. 'I hope to God it will be.'

'Helen . . .'

The urgent note in Keith's voice demanded attention. She turned back to him and the sharp, blue eyes measured her mettle.

'The smashed mirror. Will you corroborate an accident story? Any whiff of a suicide attempt could hurt Madeleine's career.'

'I'll back up any story you tell,' she assured him quickly.

He nodded and looked at Joe.

'No comment from me,' Joe answered.

'A hefty cheque will cover the damage and give the restaurant manager a heightened sense of discretion,' Keith said cynically.

So what if he was cynical, Helen thought with a sharper awareness of her own failings. Keith cared about Madeleine. They all cared, those people she had judged harshly. They had shown more humanity than she had, locked away in the private world she had made for herself. And they were generous and loyal to each other. She had been critical of them for not seeing her as a person but she had not seen them either, only the superficial trappings and talk. Only to Max had she really shown herself. And Joe . . . Joe who had known her better than anyone. Joe . . . whom she must not let go.

The *Kukuni Queen* bumped into the pier and

ground along it with a reckless disregard for paintwork.

'Action time,' Keith hissed. 'I'll hold the fort, Max. Be in touch.'

'Thanks, Keith.' As the door shut him off, Max shifted his anguished gaze to Helen. 'I'll come to your apartment when ... after ...' He faltered, too choked to go on.

'Whenever you want to, Max,' Helen rushed in, anxious to ease the difficulty of the moment. 'Please don't worry about me. Madeleine's the only person who counts right now.'

'Thanks ... thanks, Helen,' he got out huskily.

The ambulance men arrived. Helen opened the door and slipped outside so as not to be in the way. She did not watch Madeleine being lifted on to the stretcher. There was a murmur of voices, a bag clicking open and shut, the rustle of cloth; each sound impinging on her hearing yet blurred by the aftermath of shock. Reaction was setting in. Her legs shook like jelly and she had to lean against the wall for support.

At last the stretcher was carried out. Max did not even see her when he followed. His gaze was fixed on Madeleine as if he was willing his own life-force into the limp, white body. Then Joe was there in front of her and his arms slid around Helen and hugged her tightly to him. His warmth and strength enfolded her, sheltered her, soothed her. She rested her head on his shoulder and Joe rubbed his cheek against her hair and time stood still while their hearts beat in grateful unison.

They were alive. They were together. And their love had not been lost. Only mislaid.

Joe's chest rose and fell in a deep sigh and his breath whispered through her hair as he spoke. 'We'd better join the others and let Keith wrap it all up neatly. Can you hold up, Nell?'

'Yes. I'm all right now.' She lifted her head and looked up at his dear, grave face. 'Thanks, Joe.'

His mouth softened into a little smile and his eyes held a deep tenderness. 'I want to keep on holding you. May I?'

She nodded, too tongue-tied by her own feeling to speak. Joe slid his arm around her shoulders and they walked side by side back into the dining-room.

The tables had already been vacated, all except one. Dinner-guests were filing out to the gang-plank in a continuous stream. Curious eyes were turned on to the one party which remained seated. A portly gentleman with a luxurious moustache was standing by Keith, bending slightly towards him in a listening attitude. Bart Chissolm had one arm around his wife, the other stretched carelessly across the table, hand idly jiggling a glass of brandy. Jimmy had his elbow on the table, his head propped in his hand as he leaned sideways, his attention fixed on whatever Keith was saying. Cheryl and Jill were sitting stiffly upright, their faces tight and expression-less.

Keith was the first to spot Joe and Helen

approaching. He crooked a finger to bring them to his side then pushed his chair back. He stood, an imposing figure of a man as he drew a deep breath and pulled in his belly. And a powerful man, who knew how to impress his power on others. He flicked an arrogantly commanding look at the man next to him and performed a curt introduction.

'Mr Andropouli, Miss Helen Daley, Joseph Torelli.'

Quite clearly this was the manager of the restaurant. He gave a little bow and his eyes projected sympathy as he looked at Helen. 'Dear lady, a most unfortunate accident. Such a terrible shock. Can I order anything for you ... fresh coffee, some aspirin perhaps?'

'No, thank you. You're very kind but all I really want is to go home,' Helen replied, the tremor in her voice more eloquent than words.

'Yes. I understand. Then I can only express my sorrow that our restaurant will hold this unhappy memory for you.' He turned to address all of them. 'I wish you good speed home. Perhaps another time we can provide the pleasure which went so sadly astray tonight.'

It was a very smooth hint that he wanted them gone without further delay, and everyone was only too relieved to be able to comply.

They moved off in couples and no-one questioned Joe's pairing with Helen. Keith shepherded them all ahead of himself and Jill Amory. They made a silent, mournful procession as they trailed down the gangway and along the quay to the roadway. Goodnights were exchanged in a perfunctory fashion and the Danvers and Chissolms headed off towards a car-park.

Max's Rolls Royce pulled into the kerb and Barry sprang out to hold the door for Helen. Keith nodded approval and gave Barry a mock salute as he passed by, leading Jill to the chauffeured Daimler behind the Rolls. Only Joe remained beside Helen and she did not want to leave him. There was so much she wanted to say to him, words, thoughts which ached to be spoken . . . yet perhaps it was impossible to speak without inviting misunderstanding. Her sigh expressed something of her dilemma.

'Come with me, Nell.'

The words were soft, carrying only the barest inflection of urgency. Helen knew instinctively what they meant, what Joe was asking. The time for decision had come. It was a watershed in her life. To say no almost certainly meant she would never see Joe again. To say yes meant restructuring her whole life. Helen did not mind that, but Barry represented a problem.

It was not fair to Max that he should hear of her defection from his chauffeur, tonight of all nights. She hesitated, torn between the necessity of going to Joe, and the responsibility she owed to Max. She looked up at Joe for guidance but the hesitation had been too long. His eyes were dull, his face drawn into lines of resignation.

'I'll take you home, Helen.' The tone was flat,

undemanding. 'It's the sensible thing to do. The chauffeur can take the Rolls to the hospital and be on hand for Max.'

'Of course,' she muttered. It was the obvious answer and she wondered why she hadn't thought of it. She was not thinking clearly at all and she had to. It was so terribly important. Barry was still standing at attention near the passenger door. Helen addressed him in a quick, efficient voice. 'Barry, do you know what hospital Mr Abrams went to?'

'Yes, Miss Daley. St Vincent's.'

'Then I suggest you go there and wait for him. Mr Torelli has offered to drive me home and I'll go with him. Tell Mr Abrams that I'll wait up until he comes or calls that he won't be coming.'

'Very well, Miss Daley. I'll give Mr Abrams your message. Goodnight then.'

He tipped his cap and climbed into the driver's seat. The Rolls Royce purred past them and Helen watched it until it had rounded a corner and disappeared from view. She turned back to Joe. His body was as taut as a wound up spring and his eyes held a sharp watchfulness. Clearly her actions had aroused some uncertainty over her intentions. Now that they were alone she had to speak up, no matter how difficult it was to find the right words. There could be no going back on this decision.

CHAPTER EIGHT

SUDDENLY she felt afraid ... afraid with the same fear she had felt when she won the beauty contest ... the fear that communication might be beyond them. She turned her face up to him, the wide blue eyes full of vulnerable uncertainty. Joe's gaze was rock-steady, waiting, giving nothing away. It was up to her. It was she who had rejected him this time. And surely the power and pain of pride had been laid waste on the Powder Room floor of the *Kukuni Queen.*

Impulsively she reached out and took his hand, threading her fingers through his. She kept her gaze on that symbolic joining, taking courage from the way Joe had tightened the grip. She took a deep breath and forced the necessary words to her tongue.

'Joe, tonight I promised to marry another man. So it seems terrible to have to say what I have to say to you now. I can't go through with it. From the first moment I saw you tonight, you dredged up feelings that I had hoped to hide away and forget. But I couldn't hide them. And I couldn't forget. And I don't want to any more. We have something special between us that I don't think either of us will have with anyone else. After tonight, I want us to try again. If you still want me.'

She glanced up and it was there in his eyes . . . she had known instinctively that it would be. They had been separated in body but not in spirit. The body and spirit had now rejoined and the belonging was right. Undeniable.

'It was always inevitable, wasn't it, Joe?' she whispered. 'That in the end there would only be us?'

'Nell . . .'

The throb of yearning in his voice and the love in his eyes melted her bones. Her feet took the step, intuitively following a need which was older than time, the need to come home. Joe's arms came around her, drawing her in. Their hearts beat in unison, accelerating in excitement, thrumming a song of gratitude, pounding the blissful recognition of home-coming, and their kiss intensified the wonderful magic of their belonging. This was the only worthwhile reality and they clung to it, savouring it, exulting in it, holding it precious above all else. Their love did not need to be spoken. It enveloped them, bonding them into an indissolvable unit even when they drew apart.

'It's not far to the car. Are you up to walking a couple of blocks,' Joe asked in soft concern.

'Yes. I don't mind. It'll be good to walk.'

Hand in hand. It had been so long since they had done that. They had walked everywhere in their university days, rarely taking public transport. Walking used to prolong the time they had together. They had talked and talked on every subject under the sun, and beyond that, to the meaning of the universe which only had meaning because they were together. They did not talk now. Memories filled the silence, binding them in a far closer intimacy than touch or speech. They were together again.

Joe settled her into the low-slung passenger-seat. Helen was vaguely aware that the car was expensive, sporty and sleek, but she only had eyes for Joe. She watched him round the streamlined bonnet, recognised the anticipation in his lithe, springy step, was aware of the heightened sense of expectancy coursing through her own veins, and knew she wanted to share her life with him whatever the consequences. She loved him.

He slid in behind the driver's wheel and closed his door, but he did not start the car. He took her hand again, fondling it gently before lifting eyes which held an intense depth of feeling, shadowed by a flicker of uncertainty. 'You did mean it, Nell. About us . . .'

Her fingers squeezed his and her voice echoed the sense of inevitability which had accompanied her decision. 'I can no more do without you than you can do without me.'

The shadow disappeared, replaced by the warm glow of inner contentment. A wry little smile curved his lips. 'I thought . . . maybe . . . I was dreaming. All tonight has been like a nightmare. And to feel such happiness now . . .'

He shook his head and his smile broadened, as if he could not stop his joy from brimming over. 'I can hardly believe it.' His hand lifted to her hair then stroked down her cheek in a tender caress which assured him of her reality. 'Say you'll marry me, Nell.'

'I'll marry you, Joe,' she said, her voice husky with a well of emotion which brought tears to her eyes.

He leaned over and kissed her, not a kiss of passion or possession, but the lingering touch of infinite care for something uniquely precious. It was a silent, overwhelming communication of a love which transcended all else, and was theirs forever, if they so willed it.

'I don't want to look backwards, Nell,' Joe murmured, his lips still brushing hers. 'I think . . . I hope I'm a different man to the one who hurt you then. Can we go forward?'

'Yes. Oh, yes,' she whispered with heartfelt longing.

And he kissed her again, deeply, and it was a promise that nothing would ever come between them. Joe's arms slid around her, wrapping her in warm security. Helen wound her arms around his neck and they were so totally one in spirit they felt no need for more physical intimacy. For a long time they held each other, Joe's cheek rubbing lightly at her temples.

'I guess I'd better take you home,' he murmured regretfully, and began to withdraw from their embrace.

Helen was instantly reminded of Max. 'Joe . . .' She reached up and touched his cheek, an urgent appeal in her fingertips. '. . . I have to ask you to go when Max comes. It wouldn't be right not to speak to him alone. I owe him that courtesy. And . . . and he might want to talk about Madeleine.'

'It's all right, Nell,' he assured her softly. 'I understand. You're really very close, aren't you?'

'In . . . in some ways,' she agreed hesitantly. 'But not in love. That was always yours, Joe.'

He sighed and shook his head. 'Even so, I was hopelessly wrong about your relationship.'

'Yes.' She reached for words in an attempt to explain her decision to marry Max. 'We have a good understanding. There's no . . . no strong emotion getting in the way. I think, over this last year, we'd come to rely on each other. We were both lonely people and . . . it had nothing to do with wealth or position, Joe.'

'I know. I finally understood you were . . . attuned to each other's needs. And so did Madeleine. It was a very hollow feeling . . . knowing that someone else had really taken up your place.'

'No, that could never be taken up, Joe,' Helen denied swiftly. 'I haven't even slept with Max, though he's asked me often enough. I've never been with any man but you. I haven't wanted to. But tonight I gave my word to Max and I would have.' Her eyes reflected the mental agony of that decision. 'I knew it was a . . . a settling for second-best, but the best seemed out of reach.'

She sighed away the tension that the memory had brought and smiled her relief. 'I'm so glad you came, Joe. So glad it didn't happen.' She pressed her palm against his cheek, savouring the wonderful fact that she could touch this face she held so dear. 'Now I have you again.'

His hand closed over hers and drew it down to his mouth. He pressed a soft kiss on her palm, then folded her fingers over it. 'That's a promise that we'll always be in reach of each other after tonight, Nell.'

Her smile took on the beautiful serenity of inner peace. She knew it would be as Joe said. The shadow of death had touched them too closely for its lesson to ever be forgotten. Love was a gift and life was too fleeting to let it be misused or undervalued.

'Home now?' Joe asked, and the question held an underlying warmth which lent double meaning to the words.

She nodded.

He made sure the seat-belt was fastened properly and that it was comfortable for her. It gave Helen a lovely safe feeling to have Joe hovering protectively over her. He planted a soft kiss on her forehead, grinned happily as he put the car into gear, then concentrated on the road.

Helen gave him directions for the easiest route to her Mosman apartment then consciously relaxed, letting her body go entirely limp. She felt very tired but it was no longer the fatigue of too much strain. It was the happy tiredness which comes when a battle has been fought, the outcome has been favourably decided and surrender is bliss. No more decisions to be made. No uncertainty. Just a satisfied sense of utter rightness.

Helen's gaze wandered from Joe to the traffic ahead of them. It seemed like a thousand years since she had ridden into the city in the Rolls Royce with Max. She recalled the underlying panic which had mocked her confidence then. She felt no panic now. Strange that she had thought of that ride as travelling towards a new destiny. She had been right . . . and wrong. Her destiny lay with Joe. Her eyes once more drank him in, intoxicated with the sure knowledge of his love. He was hers from this time on. After tonight.

Her thoughts slid back to Max. She wished she knew what was happening with Madeleine. Max would understand about Joe but the parting would come easier if Madeleine was out of danger. Surely if Madeleine lived, Max would not let their relationship revert to the old bitter warfare. He knew now that Madeleine still loved him, so much that losing him had been unbearable. It was not too late for them to have a happy life together. If they willed it and were prepared to work at it.

Her eyes fastened on Joe again. It was not going to be easy for them either. Love had brought them back together but it would take time for a complete cementing of their relationship; time to re-adjust, time to work out the giving which was necessary to make it indestructible. Love alone could not do it. That was the lesson of the past. There had to be faith and trust and a readiness to listen and understand. No silences which hid resentments and fear. No silences! 'Joe . . .'

He glanced an inquiry at her.

'What . . . what are you thinking?'

He smiled a smile of pure exultation. 'How great it is to have you beside me.'

She relaxed again with a satisfied sigh. 'Yes it is. To have you beside me.'

'What did you think I was thinking?'

'I didn't know. I suddenly felt afraid of the silence,' she confessed ruefully.

He reached over and enclosed her hand with his. 'Don't be afraid,' he said softly. 'Don't ever be afraid of me, Nell. Always remember that I love you and don't hide any problems you have. We'll sort them out. And speaking of problems, what do you want to do about your job with Max?'

She frowned. 'I don't know. I haven't given it a thought.' She couldn't very well leave Max in the lurch, not with the Joel Thomas tour imminent. On the other hand, Max might not want her working with him after tonight's rejection. Though that was unlikely. Normally Max would put work ahead of any other consideration.

'I do realise it means a lot to you, Nell,' Joe put

in quickly. 'I'm not asking that you give it up. But I have to know what you want to do so I can organise my work around it.'

Did she want to keep her job? She would have fought tooth and nail for it earlier tonight. It had been a weighty influence on her decision to marry Max. But now? Somehow a life with Joe made the job seem insignificant. Superfluous. It had helped to fill the hole that Joe had left. She could no longer view it with the same single-minded commitment to work.

'I'll have to give Max time to replace me, and he'll be depending on me to carry through my responsibilities during the Joel Thomas tour, but I don't want to keep it on after we're married, Joe. I want the time with you.'

It was Joe's turn to frown. He shot her a worried look. 'I don't want you sacrificing a career for me. You have too much talent to be left unfulfilled in that sense. You won't be happy doing nothing, Nell. And I want you to be happy.'

'Well, I won't want such a full-time career. Not when . . .' She looked over at him hopefully. 'I'd like to have the family we once planned, Joe.'

His gaze met hers only for a moment before he returned it to the road but there were volumes spoken in that one look. Helen's heart swelled with feeling and more speech was impossible for a while. She was not afraid of this silence. It was the silence of unutterably sweet dreams.

Joe parked the car outside her apartment block

and Helen was relieved to see that Max's Rolls Royce had not arrived ahead of them. The night air seemed chill as she stepped out on to the pavement and she shivered. Joe put his arm around her shoulders, tucking her comfortably close to him as they walked inside. She was very conscious of his sleeve rubbing against her bare skin, conscious of a desire for more intimate contact which had to be choked off. Now was not the time. Not when she was expecting Max to come by. The trauma of this night was not yet over and she wanted it all behind her so that she could give herself completely to Joe.

She slid out of his hold as they entered her apartment. 'I think I'll change into warmer clothes, if you'll excuse me, Joe,' she said quickly.

He smiled, a smoky desire in his eyes. 'Yes. I guess you'd better do that. Though I do like that dress, Nell. I hope you'll wear it for me sometime.'

She looked her surprise at him. 'I thought you didn't like me wearing sexy clothes.'

He shook his head and his smile took on a little twist of self-mockery. 'I love you in sexy clothes. I just wasn't sure it was always for me. I won't make that mistake again, Nell.'

She shrugged. 'To tell you the truth, I don't really feel comfortable in them.' A self-conscious embarrassment rushed colour into her cheeks. 'I can't forget what you used to say about . . . well, you know.'

He walked over to her and cupped her burning face in his hands, the loving warmth in his eyes drawing the uncertainty from hers. 'I was a fool. I know a lot now that I didn't know then. It's just as you said, Nell. Love is not holding tight. It's letting go. No more restrictions. I want you to feel free to do as you please.'

She smiled. 'I still feel I'd like to change.'

'Then go and change. But don't be long.' He grinned. 'I'm not sure I can stand the thought of you being undressed while I twiddle my thumbs.'

Feeling ridiculously light-hearted, Helen shut herself in her bedroom and peeled off her clothes. For a moment she paused, appraising the naked body reflected in the mirror. Only Joe had ever seen her like this and suddenly she was fiercely glad that it was so. She turned to her wardrobe, a curl of irony on her lips as she recalled how she had cursed Fate for sending Joe back into her life tonight ... blessed, blessed Fate that had smiled on her, giving her back the man she loved. She quickly donned a lightweight tracksuit in a soft, caramel knit, eager to get back to him.

When she returned to the living-room, Joe was over near the shelf which had held the little china clown. Only the clown was not on its shelf. It was in Joe's hands and he was gazing down at it, a grim set to his face.

Unaccountably tears pricked Helen's eyes and once again the old grief caught at her heart. Their love might become richer and deeper, a more mature love than they had shared before, but the happy innocence of that magical day would never be theirs again.

Joe suddenly sensed her presence. He glanced up quickly and caught the poignant sadness shimmering in her eyes. Their gaze locked and Helen saw the same sadness in his. He held out the clown, carefully cradled in his hand.

'You kept it.' His voice was furred with emotion.

'I've carried it with me everywhere.'

'It was a good day.'

'The best.'

'Yes. Yes it was.'

His gaze dropped again to the clown and he gently fingered its contours, just as she had done earlier. Then in the same reflex action he thrust it back on its shelf and turned away from it. He held out his hands in a gesture which was half-apology, half-appeal.

'Maybe someday I'll give you something which will mean as much.'

'You don't have to give me things, Joe. I kept the clown because it represented love. Having your love is all I want,' she answered softly.

He came swiftly to her then, holding her in an embrace which eloquently expressed his love for her. 'Forgive me, Nell. I was so wrong about you. So terribly wrong.'

'I had my share of faults, Joe. I guess we needed to do some growing up.'

'It was a hell of a way to grow up,' he said feelingly.

She gave him a watery smile. 'Well, we made it. Here we are. We agreed not to look backwards, Joe. Let's sit down and you can tell me all your plans for the future.'

'Our plans. And I want to keep holding you, Nell.'

'I didn't say you had to stop.' She nodded towards the largest armchair. 'I think we might fit in that one.'

He grinned as he swept her up into his arms and took the couple of strides which allowed him to sit down with Helen cradled in his lap. She breathed a sigh of contentment as she wriggled to a comfortable position.

'This could very well become a refined torture,' he warned teasingly.

'Do you want me to move?'

'Hell, no! Guess I'd better talk.'

'You can tell me how terribly brilliant you are.'

'You'd better believe it!'

'Oh, I do. I'm very proud of you.'

'I'll tickle you if you keep that up. And you know where that'll lead. Once on the floor I refuse to be answerable to any consequences.'

She laughed and hung her arms around his neck. 'Seriously, Joe. I am proud of you and what you've done, all by yourself.'

His eyes beamed pleasure. 'You know the best part of it? Never having to worry where the next cent is coming from. Where would you like to live, Nell?'

'With you.'

He grinned. 'We'll take that for granted. We'll

need a big house if we're going to have kids. But first we're going to have a very long honeymoon. What do you think of hiring a crewed sailing boat and cruising down The Great Barrier Reef?'

'Sounds wonderful.' She lay her head on his shoulder and her hand worked an opening in his shirt. Her fingers found the tight black curls on his chest and idly tugged at them. 'Tell me more,' she murmured dreamily. Her thumb flicked a button free so she could spread her hand over his heart.

She felt the sharp intake of breath. His chest rose and fell under her touch. She knew she was playing with fire but could not resist the temptation of his closeness. It had been so long. So long.

Joe talked. He talked of balmy days and stopovers on islands and nights under the stars and swimming in crystal-clear waters and . . .

Her thumb flicked another button free. The flow of words stopped. Joe snatched off his tie and Helen freed his throat from all constriction. Her hand caressed the taut muscles, rediscovering the strong lines and hollows. She moved her head so that she could graze her mouth over the warm skin and breathe in the masculine scent of him.

'Nell . . . I . . .' His fingers wound through her hair and pulled her head away. Then his mouth was on hers, devouring all she would offer him with a passion which knew no bounds. His hand pushed her top up and tore his shirt open and her bare breasts were crushed against his heaving chest as he lifted her down on to the carpet.

All restraint was cast aside in the feverish need to appease a hunger which could no longer be contained. Mouths, hands, bodies strained to satisfy the fire in their blood. This was not the past or the future but now ... now ... and the desire to be one was immediate and compelling.

Helen was entirely naked, a mass of screaming nerve-ends begging to be soothed when the doorbell rang, shattering in its shrill impact. Joe was half-undressed, aroused to a pitch of frenzy, and he groaned in dire frustration as the import of that most unwelcome interruption sank in. For a moment Helen felt paralysed, then a burning wave of guilt whipped her into action.

'It's Max,' she hissed, grabbing for her clothes and pulling them back on in wild haste.

'I know. I know,' Joe muttered in anguish, re-arranging his own clothes with trembling hands.

'Tomorrow,' she promised in equal anguish.

'Yes. Tomorrow,' he breathed heavily.

The doorbell rang again. Shame scorched into Helen's cheeks. She had not given Max or Madeleine a thought this last hour and God knew what news Max was bringing. He would have been through a harrowing time at the hospital. She should have been waiting for him. Ready for him. Not making love with Joe. She smoothed her hair in agitation, hoping that her appearance did not scream of her totally wanton behaviour.

'Ready to go,' Joe declared with a crooked little smile which twisted her heart.

'Tomorrow,' she promised again, her eyes frantic with apology.

He nodded, his eyes caressing her with love. He took her arm and walked her to the door which he opened, giving Helen a moment more to compose herself for a meeting which could only be fraught with tense uncertainties.

The drawn greyness of Max's face struck panic in Helen's heart. Was Madeleine . . .

'Joe?' Max's question rose from obvious distraction.

'I brought Nell home,' came the calm explanation. 'I'll be going now you're here. How's Madeleine?'

Max dragged a hand down his face. 'I . . . I don't know. They made me leave. Said there was nothing more I could do.' He sucked in a breath and shook his head as if to clear it. 'They've given her a blood transfusion. She's in the intensive care ward. An intra-venous drip in her arm. The doctor said her condition was stable and satisfactory, whatever that might mean.'

'I'd say it means she'll pull through,' Joe said sympathetically.

Max lifted agonised eyes. 'She didn't . . . she's still unconscious. I didn't thank you for all you did, Joe. If she lives, she'll owe her life to you.'

Joe stepped forward and squeezed Max's shoulder. 'You did all you could too, Max. I'll leave you with Nell. Goodnight.' He shot one last piercing look at Helen then walked away.

There had been love and frustration in that

look and Helen had difficulty in controlling her own rampant emotion. She took Max's hand and drew him inside, very aware that he needed support, not rejection. She could not add to the lonely suffering in his eyes. This was not the time to push her own needs. She and Joe would have the future. Tonight . . . tonight she owed to Max.

CHAPTER NINE

Max's eyes darted worriedly at Helen as she closed the door. 'It was good of Joe to bring you home. You must have been in shock.' He made an agitated little gesture and turned away. 'I'm sorry, Helen.'

'It's all right, Max,' she said quickly, wanting to minimise any strain between them.

'No, it's not all right.' Shaking his head in mute denial of any rightness he dropped into the closest chair and slouched to one side, his elbow propped on the armrest as he squeezed his eyelids with finger and thumb. When he opened his eyes and looked up at her the pain had been dulled but not removed. 'I didn't know. I honestly didn't know how much . . . how deeply . . . I still felt for her. When I saw her there . . . it just broke me up, Helen.'

'You don't have to explain, Max,' she began gently. 'I understand how . . .'

'Yes, I do,' he cut in on a note of urgency. 'I do have to explain. So please, will you sit down and listen, Helen? I've got to tell you how it is. It can't wait.'

He was so up tight and obviously distressed that Helen thought it was best to stay silent and oblige him. She sank into the armchair which she and Joe had vacated and hoped Max would give her an opportunity to explain too. He stared blankly at her for a moment, then as if driven by inner torment he was on his feet again, pacing aimlessly around, rubbing the back of his neck and gesticulating with his other hand as words poured out in jerky bursts.

'It's all such a mess. I hate to disappoint you . . . embarrass you . . . it's so bloody unfair to you . . . in every way. But I have to tell you. There's no other way. I can't let her go now.'

He swung around, both hands outstretched in appeal, his eyes tortured with conflict. 'I can't let her go, Helen. I've spent ten years in an emotional desert and I've craved for the Maddie I used to have every day of those ten years. I thought she hated me. But now I know she still loves me in spite of everything I've done. I want her more than anything else in the world and if she makes it through this night, I'll be at her bedside tomorrow, begging her to marry me.' His hands made a little movement which expressed an inevitability against which any argument would be useless. 'And that's how it is.'

'I know,' Helen replied, and a soft little smile curved her mouth.

'You know?' Clearly Max was at a loss with her placid acceptance of his speech. Surprise and bewilderment chased across his face, followed by a relief which was most tangible.

Helen's relief was just as great. Max's declaration had made the situation very simple now. 'I think we all faced some hard truths in that Powder Room, Max,' she said with quiet purpose. 'I feel the same way about Joe. I don't want to live without him either. So you see, you don't have to worry about me.'

'You and Joe?' He struggled with the thought for a moment, fitting the pieces together and clinching them with the fact of Joe's presence here in her apartment. 'You've come to an understanding?'

She nodded. 'I was going to tell you but . . .'

'But I got in first.' Max sucked in a deep breath and let it out on a long sigh. His lips twisted into a curl of irony as he walked towards her. He lifted her to her feet, his hands keeping a gentle hold of her upper arms. His gaze was soft with a more tender warmth than he had shown her earlier tonight. 'I'm glad for you. You deserve the best, Helen. And I couldn't have given it to you.'

'Nor me, you,' she answered, feeling a rush of affection for him.

On mutual impulse they hugged each other tightly, instinctively giving comfort for the agony of mind both had suffered this night, and perhaps saying a silent goodbye to a relationship which had given much, promised much, but never quite enough.

'I'm going to miss you, Helen.' The murmur held the memory of the closeness they had shared.

'Only for a little while, Max. I'm replaceable.

Madeleine isn't,' she replied with the wisdom which had been so painfully learnt.

He sighed and pulled away enough to look down at her and the pain was in his eyes again. 'All those years wasted. What am I going to do if Maddie dies?'

'The doctor said her condition was stable and satisfactory. You have to believe him, Max. Think positive. That's what you always tell me.'

He made a wry grimace and his arms dropped into a dismissive wave. 'Oh, I'm so bloody sure about everything but this. It means so damned much.'

'Why don't you sit down and try to relax,' she advised. 'I'll make us some coffee. Or would you rather have a brandy?'

'No. I don't want anything,' he muttered, shaking his head as he dropped back into a chair. He waved a careless hand. 'You have a drink if you want.'

'No. I just thought . . .' She shrugged and sat down, curling herself into a comfortable position. There was more to talk about. 'What about the job, Max? We might as well get that straightened out,' she suggested quietly.

He sighed and shot her a rueful look. 'I was coming to that. I can't have you working for me, Helen. Maddie could never accept it. Not after . . .' He gestured hopelessness and ran agitated fingers through his hair. 'I don't know how I'm going to get through the next few weeks without you but I'll have to.' As if suddenly realising he was not considering Helen's position his expression changed to one of anxious apology. 'I'm sorry, Helen. I know how much you like the job.'

She was just realising that herself. The abrupt cut-off from Max was a jolt. She would have been at a terrible loose-end if she did not have Joe to turn to. And Joe had been right. She would not be content doing nothing, not having become used to the satisfaction gained by meeting the challenges involved in her work with Max. She enjoyed using her brain and her organisational skills, and the hollow disappointment she felt now emphasised her need to do so. She would have to find something else which would stretch her abilities.

Max was talking on. '... I've been wracking my brains, trying to work out how I could make it up to you. I thought of ringing Hal Beecher in London. He'd snap at the chance...'

The genial face of Hal Beecher popped into Helen's mind. He was an ex-patriate Australian, well-established in London as the agent for many top-line pop-groups and stars. He had recently hit the headlines for masterminding the production of a new, radical musical which was proving a huge success on the London stage. Working for him would carry similar responsibilities to those she had taken on for Max, but did she still want that?

'... but if you're marrying Joe...' Max hesitated, leaving the question up in the air.

And that was exactly the point. She wanted, above all, to be with Joe. 'I'll have to think about it, Max. I'm not sure what I'll do but please don't worry about me,' she added quickly, seeing his concern.

'Any help I can give you . . .'

'I know.' She smiled to assure him that she was not upset.

A small smile tugged at his mouth. 'You're not all that easily replaceable, you know.' But his eyes showed relief. It was one less hurdle in getting Madeleine back to him. He perceived Helen's understanding and the corners of his mouth turned down in wry acknowledgment. 'She's one hell of a jealous bitch, and I don't know how I'm going to live with it. But this time I'm going to make damned sure I don't give any unnecessary cause for provocation. And you're the one woman I can't possibly have near me, Helen. Not after tonight.'

She nodded, remembering Madeleine's jealous rage in the Powder Room. It had been a scene which neither woman would ever forget. Max was right to cut her out of his life. Helen could see that very clearly now. It was the only way to win Madeleine's trust and make her feel secure with his love. It was sad that it had to be so but reality rarely measured up to idealism.

She was glad that Joe had believed enough in her love to leave her alone with Max tonight. She hoped that he would never doubt it again. She looked at Max with deep compassion. Madeleine's nature would make a harder road to happiness but no-one could know that better than Max. He sat there, darkly brooding, sunk into himself, and Helen was moved to say something encouraging.

'Maybe, after tonight, she'll be more ready to believe you, Max.'

He glanced up and the torment of his thoughts was bleakly visible.

She tried to ease it. 'I mean . . . well, rejecting me to go to her. She'll know . . . she'll have to realise that you do love her . . . that you want her and not me. And since I represent everything she could be jealous of . . .' She trailed into silence because her words were not lifting Max's gloom. They seemed to have deepened it.

'It wasn't all Maddie's fault, Helen.' His mouth thinned in self-contempt. 'You know what I'm like. I've always flirted with beautiful women. It's a kick to the old ego I guess.'

He pushed himself out of the chair and wandered around restlessly as if he found it difficult to live with himself. 'I helped turn her into what she is. I used to stir her along. I enjoyed seeing her send out sparks. It made her so vivid, intensely vital. I'd taunt her into a rage, then make wild, tempestuous love to her. It was more exciting, more total than anything I've known. Before or since.'

He paused and looked at Helen with black despair. 'But I played it too far. Maybe it was the sense of power it gave me. I don't know. It was like a lever I had over Maddie. She always had such a dominant personality. In the end it all got out of hand like I told you. And now it's come to this. What if she dies?' Tears glittered in his eyes. 'What if she dies?'

Helen went to him, impulsively giving her body for whatever comfort it could offer. She held him tightly until the shuddering stopped, then slowly gentled her embrace as he regained control.

'Helen . . .' His voice was a strained croak. 'I don't want to be alone tonight. Would it be asking too much . . .'

'You can stay here, Max,' she said in quick sympathy.

'I don't mean . . .'

'I know.'

Sex was the furthest thing from his mind. He needed someone to hold on to, to share the miserable hours of waiting, to ease the frightening loneliness. Helen was aware of all this without having to be told and compassion overrode any doubts as to the wisdom of letting him stay.

'Shall I tell Barry to go?' she asked matter-of-factly.

Max shook his head. 'He's gone. I sent him home with the Rolls. I didn't know how long . . . I thought you'd be distressed and . . . I didn't know what to do,' he finished wearily.

'Well, sit down and try to relax. You've got to stop brooding over the past. It won't help, Max. You've got to look ahead and hope for the best. And on that point, we might as well spend the time working out how you'll handle the Joel Thomas tour without me.'

She persuaded him back into a chair and gradually drew him into conversation. Reluctantly at first, and then with more concentration Max responded to her suggestions. They talked around the problems until nothing more could be achieved. Silence grew and became heavy. Helen yawned. Max eyed her with rueful sympathy.

'Go to bed, Helen. I'll be all right.'

She saw the lonely shadows in his eyes and shook her head. 'I'll make us some coffee.'

She pushed herself out of the chair. Max caught her hand as she passed him and pulled her up short.

'Go on to bed,' he insisted gently. 'I'll call a taxi and go home.'

She looked down at him worriedly, feeling his need too sharply to let him go. 'You need to sleep too, Max. You'll be a nervous wreck by morning if you don't. I'm afraid I've only got one bed, but if you'd like to share it with me . . .'

His head jerked up.

A faint flush coloured Helen's cheeks at the unintentional suggestiveness of her invitation but she dismissed it with a casual shrug. 'There is comfort in company,' she added in soft sympathy.

His eyes probed hers for long moments, uncertainty slowly changing to gratitude. 'Thanks, Helen. It's . . . I've never felt so . . . so low.'

'Come on then.'

She tugged at his hand and he followed her. She turned back the bedclothes as he shrugged off his jacket. The bow-tie and the frill from his shirt had been discarded elsewhere. He hesitated and Helen gave him a little push towards the bed. With a weary sigh he climbed into it and stretched out his arm for her. Helen settled next to him, still in her tracksuit and not the least bit apprehensive that this casual intimacy could lead to any problems. Max's arm curled around her shoulders and she turned on to her side towards him, sliding an arm over his chest. They lay in silence for a while and the silence was one of mutual closeness.

'You're a good woman, Helen. I think I would've had a very contented life with you.'

'It would always have lacked something, Max,' she sighed, knowing that he had probably spoken the truth. They were very compatible in most senses.

'It's totally against reason . . . what I'm doing,' he muttered. 'If Maddie dies . . .'

'I'd still go with Joe,' Helen reminded him softly.

'Of course,' he sighed. His hand stroked her hair affectionately. 'Funny how Fate lined us up tonight. Is it going to be all right with him now?'

'I think so. Yes. Tonight was like a proving ground for us.'

'A hell of a way to prove love,' Max said harshly and sucked in a sharp breath. 'I don't think I'll ever forget the sight of all that blood.'

A deep groan tore from his throat and he turned towards her, gathering her closer and holding on in blind desperation. Helen soothingly rubbed his back until his tension eased and the uneven breathing settled into a steady rhythm again.

'Try to put it out of your mind, Max. Think of tomorrow,' she advised softly.

'Tomorrow . . .'

The word slurred out wearily and Helen kept rubbing his back, hoping the movement would relax him into sleep. Her arm gradually dragged with fatigue and her thoughts wandered to Joe. She wished she was holding him in her arms but she consoled herself with the thought that tomorrow would come soon enough and then she would always have him. It bemused her that she could be lying with a man whose physique closely matched Joe's and for whom she felt a deep affection, yet her feeling for Max could not even begin to measure against the compulsive need she had for Joe.

Her wonderful, brilliant Joe. The computer whizz. Maybe she could learn about computers. Do a course on computer programming or systems analysis. She had always been good at logic and statistics. Max might be amused by her working with dry numbers but she had liked studying economics. If she could share in Joe's business world it would make their private life so much closer. She would discuss it with him tomorrow . . . tomorrow . . . the deep sleep of utter exhaustion pulled a fog over her thoughts.

She grew vaguely conscious of a heavy weight across her waist but found it too difficult to stir herself to complete wakefulness. She tried to rid herself of the disturbing encumbrance. Only as her hand closed over a man's arm did an electric message burst into her brain.

Max! She had gone to bed with Max! They had fallen asleep. Her eyes flew open. The bright light of day made her squint. The time! My God! What was the time? She jerked her head up. Nine-o-seven. For a moment she stared at the bedside clock with disbelieving eyes, then thumped the man next to her.

'Wake up, Max! It's past nine.'

He came awake with a start, looked blankly at Helen, then snapped into full consciousness. 'Maddie! I've got to ring the hospital.'

He heaved himself off the bed and was at the telephone in the living-room before Helen made it to the kitchen. Curses of frustration accompanied his search of the directory for the right number to call. Helen put fresh coffee beans into the percolator, set it going, then hurried to the bathroom to have a quick wash and tidy herself.

The mirror reminded her that she had not creamed off last night's make-up. She looked a blotchy mess. By the time she had achieved a respectable appearance, Max had got through to a hospital official and Helen moved quietly back into the kitchen.

'. . . I was with Miss Kane last night. I accompanied her to the hospital. Now please, could you give me some information as to her condition this morning.'

There was a long pause and then a huge sigh from Max as if he had been holding his breath the whole time. 'Thank you. May I speak to her?'

There was an even longer pause and Max made a concerted attempt at wearing out the carpet around the telephone table. He stopped pacing abruptly and spoke with harsh urgency.

'Tell her it's Max. Tell her it's her Goddamned fiancé and she'd better speak to him because he's going out of his mind with worry. And repeat those exact words to her.' He heaved another sigh as he waited, grating out under his breath, 'Godalmighty! Can't she give a little?'

Then came an explosion of emotion. 'Maddie! Now just listen to me, you addle-brained woman. I love you and I'm coming over to that hospital to take you home and look after you and marry you. Have you got that? And what's more, I'm not going to listen to one bloody word you have to say because I'm taking charge of our lives right now, and there's not going to be any argument about it. No, on second thoughts, you can say two words. Say . . . yes Max.'

He expelled an exasperated breath. 'It's finished. How could it not be finished after last night? You know damned well it's you and me, Maddie. It always has been and it always will be, so just admit it to yourself and say yes Max.'

Satisfaction replaced tension. 'That's better. I'll be with you in an hour and there'll be no changing of minds because I won't stand for it. Hear me? For all of ten years I've been wanting this and I'm not going to be put off now, so hold your tongue, woman. Just lie there and think beautiful thoughts about how we're going to spend the rest of our lives. Together!'

There was a dry little chuckle. 'Just keep saying yes Max in that tone and I'll climb into the hospital bed with you.' His voice deepened and took on an edge of intensity. 'I love you, Maddie. Please don't fight me any more.'

Whatever Madeleine said had brought a smile to his tone when he added, 'You're probably right, but not today. Today we're going to be in total agreement.' He suddenly laughed. 'You're learning fast, my love. Be with you soon, Maddie. 'Bye for now.'

He put the telephone down and stood grinning at it for several moments before turning to Helen with a face which seemed boyish with happiness. 'I've got her. I've really got her,' he said exultantly, and with a few strides he was in the kitchen and whirling Helen around in his elation.

She laughed at him, delighted that everything had worked out happily. 'You were very masterful. Congratulations!'

His laugh bubbled with triumph. 'It's the only way with Maddie. Hit her when she's weak. That women has a will of iron.'

He said it with pride and his eyes sparkled with

anticipation of all the challenges that Madeleine would hurl at him ... not with malice now ... but simply because it was her nature to challenge ... an exciting, complex woman who would always hold Max in thrall. He would not even see that she was thin and angular and not particularly fashionable. She was Maddie. And he loved her.

He let Helen go and was off to the telephone again, charged with his usual dynamic energy. 'I must ring Barry to bring me a change of clothes post-haste. Have you got a shaver I can use, Helen?'

'Mmh. In the bathroom cabinet. You're welcome to it. The coffee's almost ready, Max. Do you want some breakfast?' she asked as he began to dial again.

'No, thanks. Coffee'll be fine. Did I tell you you're a marvellous woman?'

She laughed. Everything was marvellous. Max had Madeleine. Joe was coming today and life would not be lonely any more. Not for her or Joe or Max or Madeleine. It was going to be a wonderful, wonderful day.

She made herself some toast and poured out the coffee. Max emerged from the bathroom, the shine of his happiness beaming off his freshly-shaven chin. He kissed her cheek in sheer exuberance as she handed him a mug of coffee.

'Thanks, Helen. Thanks for being all you've been to me. And I hope Joe makes you very, very happy.'

A wave of sentiment almost choked her. 'I

hope you'll be happy too, Max. If you don't mind, I'll go and have a shower and get changed. When will Barry be here?'

Max glanced at his watch. 'Ten minutes or so.'

'Be out by then. Turn the radio on if you like.'

He grinned. 'I think I'll just think thoughts. I've got great thoughts this morning.'

Helen had some great thoughts herself as she soaped her body under the shower. She was remembering the exciting touch of Joe's hands, the sensual pleasure he could arouse with the lightest caress, and her blood tingled in anticipation. They had not made a time for him to come today but she expected that he would wait until eleven o'clock or so. It had been almost two o'clock when he had left last night and he would have realised that her talk with Max would take some time.

But not all night. She frowned, wondering if she should tell Joe that Max had stayed the night with her. Yes, he would understand, she decided, particularly when she told him about Madeleine. Besides, she did not want to have secrets from Joe. Her darling, beautiful Joe.

She smiled as she towelled herself dry and applied a liberal sprinkling of her favourite Arpege talcum. She slipped her arms into the richly embroidered silk kimono and wrapped it around her. Perhaps she should leave this on over her nakedness, she thought wickedly, then grinned at her wanton thoughts. After the frustration of their interrupted love-making last night she was feeling distinctly primitive.

The doorbell rang as she fastened the tie-belt. Barry had obviously laid a heavy foot on the accelerator to get here so quickly. She would have to wait to get dressed now, if she decided to do so at all. Max would want the use of the bedroom. She emerged from the bathroom and headed towards the kitchen, thinking to have another cup of coffee, while Max changed. He was just opening the front door. Helen hurried her pace, a little self-conscious about Barry's seeing her in her robe, especially since he would assume that Max's stayover was far from innocent.

But it was not Barry at the door. It was Joe. And she froze in mid-step, a crawling horror prickling her skin as his expression underwent a frightening change.

CHAPTER TEN

No! No! Don't think it, Joe! Please don't! her brain screamed in protest. Her mouth opened to deny what was so clearly written on Joe's face but her tongue would not move. She stared helplessly back at the sickened eyes in the pale, taut face.

It was Max who spoke. 'I didn't sleep with Helen, if that's what you're thinking, Joe. At least I did, but . . .'

He got no further. A savage glitter had leapt into Joe's eyes. His jaw clenched belligerently and a fist swung. Max grunted in pain as he doubled over, hugging the punched stomach as he fought for breath.

'That's for Madeleine!' Joe grated out, eyeing Max with bitter contempt. His gaze lifted to Helen and the bleak wintriness of that gaze froze her soul.

He stood there, stiffly proud, and despite all the anguished messages screeching from her brain, Helen could not speak. Her tongue seemed rivetted to the roof of her mouth.

Joe's lips curled in disgust. 'You make me sick. How could you do it? To Madeleine. And to me. I hope you both screwed beautifully because you've screwed me up for the last time. Goodbye, Helen.' He gave the name his full contempt then turned on his heel to leave. He took one pace, halted and swung back to her, his face no longer a bitter mask but fighting a conflict which was tearing him apart. 'Was it worth it, Nell? Was he so much a better lover than I am?'

And on that note of wrenching pain he turned and left. Only then did Helen's paralysis shake free. She rushed forward in a desperate attempt to stop Joe but Max stumbled ahead of her, blocking her way.

'Come back, you bloody fool!' he roared, then groaned at the forced expulsion of breath before biting out a command. 'Stop him, Barry!'

Helen dodged past Max, her heart thumping wildly as she ran to the balustrade at the head of the stairs. Barry had Joe blocked on the first landing and the two men were pushing at each other.

'No one could be better than you, Joe,' she cried vehemently. 'No one but you could make me happy.'

His head jerked up, eyes searching and finding hers, the physical struggle with Barry forgotten as hope and despair fought their silent battle in his soul.

'Fetch that case up here, Barry,' Max said brusquely. 'And for your information, Joe, I'll be on my way to Madeleine as soon as I've changed into fresh clothes. I happened to have slept in the clothes I'm wearing and neither I nor Helen thought for one moment of taking them off. She's your woman, if you've got the sense to keep her!

And Maddie's mine!' He glared his disgust at Joe then took the case from Barry. 'Wait in the car. I'll be down in a minute.'

'Yessir, Mr Abrams,' was Barry's perky response. He exhibited a lively curiosity in the whole tableau as he made a slow retreat.

Joe had not moved. Nor did he move when Max walked back into the apartment with the case of clothes. His eyes clung to Helen's as if mesmerised by the desperate plea she was projecting so urgently. The stricken look on his face grew more deeply etched. His throat moved convulsively.

'What have I done?' The hoarse whisper broke from his lips. His chest heaved as if fighting nausea and his gaze abruptly dropped. He shook his head and ran a trembling hand through his hair. 'My God! What have I done?' he repeated in an appalled mutter.

'Please come up, Joe,' Helen begged, uncaring of anything he'd done as long as he came back to her.

He lifted horrified eyes. 'I didn't believe in you. I let the circumstances damn you ... unheard. How could I do that ... after last night? I thought I'd grown past such ...'

'Joe, it doesn't matter,' she pleaded urgently. 'I don't care. I love you. Please come up and let's go inside. I want you, Joe. No-one else. No-one else in the world.'

He came. Slowly. As if each step hurt him. She slid her arms around his waist. He looked down at her with tormented eyes then crushed her to him in a fiercely possessive embrace, one arm almost encircling her while the other hand thrust through her hair and pressed her head on to his shoulder. He spoke in agonised little bursts.

'I must be mad. I swore I'd never doubt your love again. And I threw it all away. Just like last time.'

'But you listened, Joe. You came back,' she reassured him from a grateful heart.

'It's not good enough for you, Nell. It's just not good enough.'

She eased back a little to smile her love up at him. 'It'll do. For starters. Now kiss me, Joe. It's been a long time since you left.'

'Oh, Nell,' he groaned, but she reached up and smothered the sound with her own lips.

Barely a heartbeat later Joe's mouth was devouring hers with passionate need and Helen held nothing back in her response, driven by the same urgent desire for a reassurance of love.

'Hmmm ... She certainly never kissed me like that.'

They broke apart to find Max standing in the doorway, smartly attired in fresh clothes and wearing a lightly mocking smile. He held up a warning hand.

'And don't punch me again, Joe. I think I've got a glass stomach.'

'I'm sorry, Max,' Joe said stiffly, still uncomfortable with having been so wrong.

'Forget it.' Max's smile turned a little wry. 'I

blew it just like that with Maddie ten years ago, only I kept walking. This time it's going to take dynamite to shift me. She's fine, by the way.'

'I know. I rang the hospital first thing this morning.'

Max's eyes measured Joe for a long moment before he spoke, and then his words carried pointed emphasis. 'You asked me last night if I appreciated the woman Helen is. I hope you do, Joe. Last night I needed a friend and she stood by me. I'd give her my trust if I were you, because a more loyal woman you'll never find. I regret, very much, that our friendship must end today, but I must give my loyalty to the woman I love. I wish you both every happiness.'

He offered his hand and Joe gripped it hard. 'Thanks, Max. All the best to you too.'

Max smiled and nodded. He turned to Helen. His hand lightly gripped her shoulder as he kissed her forehead. 'Thanks again, Helen. Let me know if I can help with a job. I'll always be your friend, even if we never see each other again.'

'I know. Good luck, Max,' she said softly, tears of sentiment pricking her eyes.

'Same to you. Goodbye, Helen.' He gave her shoulder a light squeeze and then he was off, clattering down the stairs in his haste to get to Madeleine.

Helen was sharply aware that the dying echo of Max's footsteps rang the closing curtain on a phase of her life. For a moment she regretted the inevitable parting of the ways. But then she looked up at Joe and knew that whatever the future brought, she would not trade it for anything else.

His face still showed marks of strain as she drew him inside her apartment. Wanting to ease his mind completely, Helen began on a matter-of-fact explanation of the scene which had been so nearly catastrophic.

'I wasn't expecting you this early. Max was waiting on Barry to come so I thought I'd have a shower and get dressed ready for you. I was just out of the bathroom when the doorbell rang, so I decided to leave the bedroom free for Max and . . .'

'Don't!' Joe shut the door behind them with an impatient snap which punctuated the command. He pulled her into his arms and the dark intensity of his eyes pleaded for a cessation of all misunderstandings. 'Don't be defensive with me, Nell. I hate myself enough as it is.'

'I don't want you to hate yourself,' she replied earnestly. 'I love you, Joe. I know how bad it must have looked to you.'

An ironic smile curled his mouth and one hand slid caressingly around her throat. His eyes held a gentle self-mockery. 'No, it didn't look bad. It looked too good. Even as I was shooting off my mouth I wanted you like hell.' He heaved a rueful sigh and the thwarted desire which had wreaked such havoc, sprang to vibrant life in his eyes.

'I want you too,' she whispered invitingly.

His other hand came up and he gently cupped her face while his eyes searched hers intently, assuring himself that they held no reservation. Freed from the inhibitions of his own making he kissed her deeply, with a slow sensuality which sent a prickling awareness racing through Helen's veins. She moved closer, pressing her body to his, and with only that slight encouragement Joe reacted sharply, his hands dropping to her lower back and thrusting her forward to drive her softness against the rock-hard muscles of his masculinity.

He wrenched his mouth from hers, gasping in breath as his hands kneaded her rounded flesh to an acute awareness of his arousal. The heat of her own arousal melted her bones so that she was totally pliant to his touch. Her hands worked up under the cotton-knit shirt he had worn and fingered their way over the rippling muscles of his back, digging, caressing, glorying in the hard, male strength of him.

'Oh, God! Nell! I need you now. Now!'

'Yes,' she breathed, her whole body aching to answer his need.

He was sliding the robe from her shoulders even as she urged him towards the bedroom. It slithered to the floor and she stepped over it before turning to him and lifting his shirt so that his nakedness could meet hers. But the satisfaction she craved was not met until Joe rid himself of all clothes and then the erotic intensity of heated flesh moving against heated flesh incited an overwhelming need for immediate possession.

As Joe's first thrust sent its devastating wave of sensation through her body, Helen moaned with pleasure. It seemed that every cell awoke to sweet remembrance . . . this was her man, her mate, her other half, and she welcomed him back with all her being, instinctively riding with his rhythm and wantonly urging a tempest of physical savagery which pounded its message of exultant possession to a climax of shuddering ecstasy.

Then they clung to their inner world of melting together, hearts gradually slowing to a beat of blissful peace, mouths and eyes caressing each other with the warm tenderness of love which has been given total satisfaction.

'This is when you look most beautiful, Nell,' Joe murmured, a touch of smug pride enriching his pleasure.

She smiled, moving her body languorously against his. 'You make me feel beautiful.'

He grinned, a happy grin which was completely free of all the tension which had existed between them. 'I dreamed of this last night, but dreams are a poor shadow of reality, Nell. To be with you like this . . . if I died right now, I wouldn't be discontent with what I've had.'

'Don't you dare die on me, Joe. I've only just started to live.' She sighed in glorious contentment, tracing the happy lines around his eyes with a soft finger. 'I dreamt of you too. I wished you had not needed to go last night. I wanted you so much.'

He gave a wry little laugh. 'Never in the history of mankind has a man had to exert so much control to do the right thing as I did last night. I could have cheerfully killed Max as I said goodnight.' He sighed and shook his head. 'And to think I almost blew it this morning.' He rolled on to his back, pulling her with him so that her body covered his. 'To think I could've missed this . . . missed you . . .'

She placed a silencing hand across his mouth while her eyes denied any such disaster. 'I wasn't going to let you get away, Joe. Shock had me stumped for a few moments but I would've come after you if you hadn't come back. We would've sorted it out in the end. It had to be.'

'You would've come? Even after what I said to you?' he quizzed wonderingly.

She smiled, cutting away this last thread of insecurity. 'Either that or live alone for the rest of my life. And I've had enough loneliness. You're the only man for me, Joe.'

'And I'm your slave,' he said softly. 'I have been ever since we first met. I resented the power you had over me, Nell. And fought against it. But now . . . now I know that all I really want is to make you happy. To see you smile. To give you pleasure. To love you with all that I am.' He rolled her back so that he leaned over her. 'And that, my beautiful Nell, is what I'm going to do right now. All for you this time. Lie there. Just lie there and let me love you.'

It was difficult at first, merely to accept and not return the caresses, but Joe was insistent.

'Just watching you respond is exciting enough,' he declared, his gaze sweeping the erected nipples of her breasts before lowering his mouth to them.

Never before had Helen abandoned herself so totally to the exquisite persuasion of touch and the pleasure Joe had always given her took on more delicate nuances, different levels, deeper sensations, and her body was alive within itself, pulsating with excitement, quivering with anticipation, nerve-ends leaping in fierce delight. She heard herself moaning, crying out as the fine-tuned awareness of pleasure stretched to unbearable tension.

'Enough! Enough, Joe, please,' she begged, writhing helplessly in her need for the union which would take her into the blissful contentment she had always known with him.

She shuddered convulsively as he entered her and let out her tortured breath in a grateful sigh. But Joe was not intent on quick satisfaction. He was savouring the control she had ceded to him and each deliberate stroke of penetration was even more tantalising than all the erotic foreplay. Her tension increased, built on to by wave after wave of intense pleasure, exploding through her with such force that she ached from it. She could hardly breathe as Joe drove her closer to an unimaginable brink.

It was as if her whole body was about to gell into an amorphous mass which would change the

very essence of what she had been and for a
moment fear urged that she retreat from that
brink. 'No . . . no . . .' They were weak gasps,
breaking from a mind which was almost
incoherent.

'Don't fight it. Go with it.'

She heard him. It was Joe taking her to this
unknown place, Joe who was leading her over
into something new, and she could feel him
flowing with her. There was nothing to fear. She
opened her eyes and there he was, so dominant,
so sure, and the pain did not matter. She gave
herself up to his keeping, forever abandoning the
singleness of self to the dependence of love. What
little strength she had left seeped away and she
lay limp, entirely at Joe's mercy, conscious only
of a rising tide of pain which suddenly peaked
and shot out sprays of exquisite relief. So intense
was that ecstatic flood of feeling that Helen lost
herself in it. Her mind floated down a dizzying
well of sensation which gently receded into
nothingness.

'Nell . . . Nell . . .'

The urgent note of Joe's voice reached her,
tugging her back to him. She felt his hands on
her face, anxiously pleading for attention. She
opened eyes which mirrored the stunning depth
of the feeling inside her. His face swam into
focus. Her Joe . . . and she was his woman . .
now and forever.

'Are you all right?'

Beautifully all right. Incredibly all right. She

tried to lift her arm. The movement came sluggishly. Strange how disembodied she felt. Still floating. But the arm obeyed the need to reach Joe, to smooth the anxious lines from his forehead. She smiled as his face cleared and her eyes communicated more eloquently than any words that he was the ruler of her world. 'Not a slave, Joe,' she whispered.

He smiled. 'Yes, I am, Nell, but you make me feel like a king too, so I am content. More than content, my love. Riding on Cloud Nine with every silver lining beaming directly on me. On us.'

Her hand curled around his neck and pulled his head down to lie next to hers. She brought her other arm up and trailed a possessive path down his spine to the small of his back. 'Don't ever leave me, Joe,' she murmured huskily. 'Only you can give me this life.'

His lips brushed her ear. 'As long as you live I'll be at your side. Nothing could ever separate me from you now.'

And Helen knew he spoke the truth, the ultimate truth which would stand against all the trials and tribulations which Fate could possibly contrive to test their love, because they were one and the same being, an entity . . . complete.

She sighed and closed her eyes.

'Don't go to sleep, Nell,' Joe whispered, feathering her cheek with his lips. 'We can't let today slip by on us.'

'What do you want to do?' she asked, moving her body in a languorous tease.

He chuckled and dropped a light kiss on her mouth. 'I don't think I'm capable of topping that, Nell. You'll have to stay satisfied for a while.'

She smiled. 'I'm satisfied. I just want to hang on to you.'

'And I want to hang on to you. That's why I want us to go and buy a ring. The most ostentatious damned ring that will fit on your finger so that everyone who sees it will know how much I love you.'

Rings were only symbols, Helen thought uncaringly. It was what they had now that was important. But she understood the exuberance of feeling behind Joe's proposal. He wanted to see her wearing his ring and she would wear it with pride because it was the symbol of his love.

'In a little while, Joe,' she proposed. 'But for now, just hold on to me.'

And he did. With joy. With love. With laughter. With tenderness. And their contentment grew, forever banishing loneliness to time past. They had come home.

Harlequin Presents

Coming Next Month

887 LOVE ME NOT Lindsay Armstrong
A schoolteacher prepares to lead on an Australian boat designer. That's what he did to her sister, after all! But she doesn't count on his infinite charm—and her sister's deceit!

888 THE WINTER HEART Lillian Cheatham
After taking the blame for her sister's tragic carelessness, an artist escapes to Colorado to work as a secretary—never dreaming that her new boss chose her specifically.

889 A VERY PRIVATE LOVE Melinda Cross
While covering an Egyptian Arabian horse show in Kentucky, a reporter traveling incognito uncovers a reclusive American entrepreneur, also in disguise. He's the man she's been waiting for—to make or break her future.

890 THE OVER-MOUNTAIN MAN Emma Goldrick
A motorist stranded in the Great Smoky Mountains seeks refuge at the home of an inventor who imagines she's in cahoots with his aunt to end his bachelor days. What a notion....

891 THE MAN IN ROOM 12 Claudia Jameson
What with the blizzard and the flu epidemic at her mother's Welsh country inn, the man in room twelve is too much. And for the first time in her life, Dawn loses control of her emotions.

892 DARKNESS INTO LIGHT Carole Mortimer
The security-conscious new owner of the Sutherland estate warns his gardener against falling in love with him. But the only danger she can see is that he might break her heart....

893 FOREVER Lynn Turner
Can a surly ex-army colonel and a bogus nun find love and lasting happiness? Perhaps, with the help of a guardian angel to get them through the jungle alive!

894 A MOMENT IN TIME Yvonne Whittal
The shock of seeing each other again shatters the composure of a divorced couple. For her, at least, love lasted longer than a moment in time, though she isn't so sure of him.

Available in June wherever paperback books are sold, or through Harlequin Reader Service.

In the U.S.
901 Fuhrmann Blvd.
P.O. Box 1397
Buffalo, N.Y. 14240-1397

In Canada
P.O. Box 2800, Postal Station A
5170 Yonge Street
Willowdale, Ontario M2N 6J3

Can you keep a secret?

You can keep this one plus 4 free novels

WORLDWIDE LIBRARY IS YOUR TICKET TO ROMANCE, ADVENTURE AND EXCITEMENT

Experience it all in these big, bold Bestsellers— Yours exclusively from WORLDWIDE LIBRARY WHILE QUANTITIES LAST

To receive these Bestsellers, complete the order form, detach and send together with your check or money order (include 75¢ postage and handling), payable to WORLDWIDE LIBRARY, to:

In the U.S.
WORLDWIDE LIBRARY
901 Fuhrmann Blvd.
Buffalo, N.Y. 14269

In Canada
WORLDWIDE LIBRARY
P.O. Box 2800, 5170 Yonge Street
Postal Station A, Willowdale, Ontario
M2N 6J3

Quant.	Title	Price
_____	**WILD CONCERTO**, Anne Mather	$2.95
_____	**A VIOLATION**, Charlotte Lamb	$3.50
_____	**SECRETS**, Sheila Holland	$3.50
_____	**SWEET MEMORIES**, LaVyrle Spencer	$3.50
_____	**FLORA**, Anne Weale	$3.50
_____	**SUMMER'S AWAKENING**, Anne Weale	$3.50
_____	**FINGER PRINTS**, Barbara Delinsky	$3.50
_____	**DREAMWEAVER**, Felicia Gallant/Rebecca Flanders	$3.50
_____	**EYE OF THE STORM**, Maura Seger	$3.50
_____	**HIDDEN IN THE FLAME**, Anne Mather	$3.50
_____	**ECHO OF THUNDER**, Maura Seger	$3.95
_____	**DREAM OF DARKNESS**, Jocelyn Haley	$3.95
_____		

YOUR ORDER TOTAL	$_____	
New York and Arizona residents add appropriate sales tax	$_____	
Postage and Handling	$___.75	
I enclose	$_____	

NAME _____

ADDRESS _____ APT.# _____

CITY _____

STATE/PROV. _____ ZIP/POSTAL CODE _____

WW-1-3

One of America's best-selling romance authors writes
her most thrilling novel!

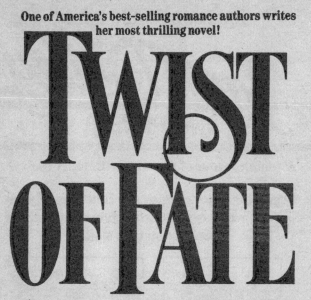

TWIST OF FATE

JAYNE ANN KRENTZ

Hannah inherited the anthropological papers that could
bring her instant fame. But will she risk her life and give
up the man she loves to follow the family tradition?